Roxey's Eyes Sparked With Anger.

"May I use the phone?" she asked.

Seth folded his arms and looked down at her. "We don't have one."

Her shoulders sagged in defeat. "I should've known. Anyone who would live in this godforsaken place wouldn't want a phone. So how am I supposed to get back to town?"

"Sounds like a personal problem to me, lady." He turned and walked toward the door.

She stopped him with a firm grip on his forearm. "I came here at your request. So that makes it *your* problem, too."

He paused and looked down at her manicured hand. Then at her. "Maybe."

"Maybe *what*?" she demanded.

"Maybe it's my problem, too," he replied slowly.

Roxey was tempted to slap that smug look off his face. "You are a rude, overgrown, slow-minded—" she sucked in air through tight lips, tryin~~~ come up with a word insult~~~ him "—mule!"

Dear Reader:

It's summertime, and I hope you've had a chance to relax and enjoy the season. Here to help you is a new man—Mr. August. Meet Joyce Thies's *Mountain Man*. He thinks he's conquered it all by facing Alaska, America's last frontier...but he hasn't met his mail-order bride yet!

Next month will bring a special man from Dixie Browning. Mr. September—Clement Cornelius Barto—is an unusual hero at best, but make no mistake, it's not just *Beginner's Luck* that makes him such a winner.

I hope you've been enjoying our "Year of the Man." From January to December, 1989 is a twelve-month extravaganza at Silhouette Desire. We're spotlighting one book each month with special cover treatment as a tribute to the Silhouette Desire hero—our *Man of the Month*!

Created by your favorite authors, these men are utterly irresistible. Don't let them get away!

Yours,

Isabel Swift
Senior Editor & Editorial Coordinator

PEGGY MORELAND
A Little Bit Country

Silhouette Desire

Published by Silhouette Books New York

America's Publisher of Contemporary Romance

For my grandmother, Myrtie Bozeman,
who encouraged me
to cast my dreams among the stars,

and

For my husband, Frederick,
who allowed me the freedom
to pursue those dreams

SILHOUETTE BOOKS
300 East 42nd St., New York, N.Y. 10017

ISBN: 0-373-05515-3

First Silhouette Books printing August 1989

Printed in the U.S.A.

PEGGY MORELAND

met her husband on a blind date during her senior year in college. Both native Texans, after nine moves in thirteen years of marriage, they have learned to look at her husband's transfers as "extended" vacations. Each move has required a change of careers for Peggy: high school teacher, real-estate broker, accountant, antique-shop owner. Now living in Oklahoma with her husband and three children, Peggy is working on a master's degree in creative studies while doing what she loves best—writing!

Dear Reader,

Home schooling is an accepted and viable alternative to public school education, but one which requires a strong commitment from the parents who choose it.

Roxanne Classen's position no longer exists within the state of Kentucky. In order for Seth and Roxey to meet, I recreated her job and assigned her duties that would necessitate her interviewing the Dandridge family.

I hope you enjoy reading Roxey and Seth's story as much as I have enjoyed sharing it with you. And perhaps in reading it, you, too, will discover you are *A Little Bit Country*.

One

Clouds of dust billowed behind Roxanne Classen's BMW as it bumped along the deeply rutted country road. Within the steamy interior of the car, perspiration beaded her forehead, dampening the copper curls at her temples and bringing her temper to near boiling point. If there was one thing Roxanne despised about summer, it was the heat. She'd only just come to this realization, for she'd never dealt with heat before. In the past if she'd been hot, she would have cooled off in her backyard pool, or wiled away the hottest hours in her air-conditioned home, or maybe even escaped by plane to a cooler climate.

But this summer was different. She shot the car's useless air conditioner a baleful look, and for good measure whacked the dashboard above it with her fist. Neither action worked. The air conditioner continued its futile whine, and the air blowing through it remained warm and stifling. For a moment she was tempted to press the button to lower the window, but a glance in the rearview mirror at the dust chasing her bumper quickly changed her mind.

Well, she could take the heat and at the same time prove to her father she wasn't some useless female. Heading charitable committees and marrying "right" might've been enough for her mother and her sister, but they weren't enough for Roxey. She had a mind and she intended to use it, even if it meant working at this plebeian job for a year in order to prove to her father her determination to take a place in the family business.

With her mind focused on the unfairness of being born a female, she didn't see the pothole until it was too late. The right front tire bounced into it with a bone-jarring thud and out of it with Roxey gripping the steering wheel to keep the car on the road.

Why in God's name would anyone want to live this far from a real road? she thought in frustration. She would take the city any day. Paved streets, curbs, sidewalks. Even at their worst, they beat this cow path she was driving on.

Out of the corner of her eye, she spotted a rabbit darting from the camouflaging weeds that grew beside the road and out onto the hard-packed dirt in front of her. Without thought to her own safety, she slammed on the brake and jerked the steering wheel to the left. The car slid toward the shallow ditch with Roxey fighting for control. With a jolt that threw her upper body into the steering wheel and her head against the side window, the left tire careened over the edge of the narrow road and hit the bottom of the ditch.

After a moment Roxey raised her arms to cradle the top of the steering wheel and pressed her damp forehead against the back of her hands. Five years busting her rear end to earn bachelor's and master's degrees and for what? A hot, sweaty, thankless job approving parents for home schooling. Not the plush surroundings of the family-owned bank she'd dreamed of, but instead hot, bumpy road's surrounded by—she lifted her head and glanced around—barbed-wire fences, dumb cows and a sea of blue-green grass. Nothing. She was surrounded by nothing.

She cocked her head to look out the passenger window in time to see the white cottontail disappear into the tall weeds at her right. Well, at least she hadn't hit Thumper. Her relationship with animals was limited to Walt Disney movies. To her every rabbit was Thumper, just as every deer was Bambi, and though she would have tried to hide it, it would have devastated her to kill one of her favorite cartoon characters—even unintentionally.

Roxey shouldered the car door open and stepped out. Her open-toed shoes immediately filled with grit. Perched like a flamingo, she shook her foot and frowned at the sand and pebbles cascading from the opening at her toes. She took a tentative step, and a thorn-riddled vine snagged her hose. Another step and she felt the runner climb all the way to her thigh.

"I am *not* going to let this get to me," she threatened no one in particular and the countryside in general. She squatted down at eye level with the hub cap.

"Great," she mumbled in a defeated voice. It didn't take a genius to see it would take a wrecker to pull the car back onto the road.

Standing, she lifted one hand to shade her eyes and fitted the other in a tight fist at her waist. The road she'd been driving on snaked in lazy curves to disappear into a low valley. About two miles below her, a chimney peeked through a cluster of pine trees. According to the directions she'd been given, she determined the chimney must belong to the Dandridges' home. Resigned to the long, hot walk that awaited her, Roxey slung the strap of her purse over her shoulder, grasped the handle of her leather briefcase and set off down the road.

Grasshoppers bounced off her legs while gnats buzzed around her face. The constant hum of insects—both seen and unseen—drove her crazy. That was what she hated about the country, she decided. There wasn't enough noise. From the pasture at her left, a cow bawled. Roxey shot her a frown. *People* noise, she clarified.

If she were in the city, there would be the scream of sirens, the blare of a car's horn and music pulsing from the jam box of some teenage rock fan.

And a telephone booth. At this point she would have given almost anything to let her fingers do the walking for a while.

Anger and frustration bent her body forward at a seventy-degree angle, the briefcase jerking forward to waist level and then back as she marched down the road. God help the Dandridges when she arrived. Roxey wasn't quick to anger, but when she was mad, those who knew her kept out of her way.

Dust kicked up from the dry roadbed left her face feeling gritty and parched, while the hot afternoon sun glared down, making her scalp perspire beneath the weight of her thick hair. Her anger carried her on long after the sun had sapped her energy.

The next time she received an application from someone in the rural area, they could darn well come to her office.

Where was the old bag? The second cutting of hay lay in the fields, the north fence needed mending and the door on the well house needed repair. Seth Dandridge stopped his pacing in front of the fireplace and glanced up at the mantel clock for the third time in as many minutes. He had work to do. Her letter said one-thirty and it was after two o'clock. Some people had no respect for time.

In the summer months, time was of the essence to Seth. As a farmer he worked a tight schedule, and this old lady was playing havoc with it. He didn't have time for a tea party with some old frump from the education department. And why did he need the state's approval to teach his kids at home anyway? Hell, they were his kids. He ought to have the right to teach them himself if he wanted to.

With his hands at the waist of his faded jeans, he strode to the screen door and glared out at the road leading up to his house. Something caught his eye and he straightened, then leaned forward for a better look. A young woman limped down the road toward the house. Puffs of dust followed her, kicked up by the purse she dragged through the dirt behind her. Her right shoulder sagged under the weight of the briefcase clutched in her hand.

He palmed the screen door open, strode to the top of the porch steps and leaned a shoulder against the cedar support post. With his arms crossed and his hands flattened under his armpits, he tried to hide a smug smile as he watched the young woman struggle toward the house. Perspiration circled her silk dress under her arms. Dust covered what looked to him to be designer shoes. Her hose were snagged and sagging at the ankles. His gaze followed a thin runner up her leg until it disappeared under the hem of her dress—and he wished he could see more. What a pair of legs!

He glanced up at what might once have been a stylish hairdo and worked his way down her body again, a frown wiping away all traces of his earlier smugness. If she washed off the dust and brushed her hair, he knew what he would find. A city slicker of all people!

Roxey tucked in her upper lip and blew up at her bangs. She closed her eyes and dropped her briefcase with a decided thump and began to wiggle her numb fingers. The release of the heavy weight sent tingles of pain shooting up her arm, and she hugged it to her waist and rubbed it with her other hand. She couldn't take much more. Her head was throbbing, her feet were killing her, and her mouth was as dry as the wind kicking up dust devils at her feet.

Her gaze slowly traveled up the steps leading to the porch. *Just a few more steps, Roxey. You can do it.* Then her thoughts froze as she locked eyes with the meanest-looking man she'd ever had the misfortune to meet. He glared at her through narrowed eyes as dark and forbidding as her grandmother's black onyx dinner ring.

The man had the size and, judging by the scowl on his face, the disposition of a grizzly bear woken early from a long winter nap. His chest under his crossed arms strained at the blue cotton work shirt, and his biceps bulged beneath the carefully rolled sleeves.

Roxey should have been intimidated by the height of the man, but she wasn't. She bent at the knees, grasped the handle of her briefcase and climbed the steps, thinking if the mountain wouldn't come to Mohammed, Mohammed would go to the mountain.

Roxey stepped onto the porch and dropped her briefcase at her feet. Maybe she could teach this country bumpkin a few manners. Using those she'd reluctantly learned at finishing school, she extended her right hand. "How do you do. I'm Roxanne Classen."

Seth glanced down at the extended hand and focused on bright red nail polish and an emerald-cut diamond ring that probably cost as much as his new tractor. Not just a city slicker, they'd sent a *rich* city slicker.

He grasped her hand in a bone-crushing grip. "'Bout time." He saw her wince, and realizing the fragility of the small hand clasped in his, he loosened his grip and slowly pumped her arm up and down.

Strength and power lay in the hand holding Roxey's—and something more. Nerve tingles worked their way up her arm—tingles she couldn't attribute to the weight of the heavy briefcase.

She pulled her hand from his. "I'm sorry for the inconvenience. There was a rabbit on the road, and when I swerved to miss it, my car slid off into the ditch."

Seth frowned again. If she expected compassion from him she would damn well be disappointed. He'd already lost two hours out of his workday because of her and wasn't about to waste any more time listening to some half-cocked woman's excuses.

Seth towered over her, scowling as he watched her brush the dust from her dress. He'd expected a middle-aged, dowdy woman with gray hair and a spinster's bun, not this young slip of a thing fresh from the country club. He was having a hard time concealing his frustration. Shoot, the woman wasn't much bigger than his ten-year-old son.

Her movements were quick and sure as she reached for her briefcase, and when she straightened and looked up at him, her eyes sparked an unspoken challenge. Roxanne Classen might be small in stature, but Seth quickly decided that was the only insignificant thing about her. Where he'd expected to find a tightly wound bun, copper-colored hair kinked out all over and curled in varied lengths to her shoulders. And judging by the way she squared her shoulders and met his scowling gaze with one of her own, he knew he was dealing with a spitfire.

"If you'll be so kind as to introduce me to Mrs. Dandridge, we'll get started." Roxey turned to walk to the front door.

He followed her and reached around her to pull it open. "There *is* no Mrs. Dandridge."

His ice-coated words halted Roxey in midstride. She glanced back over her shoulder, her eyebrows pulled together, wrinkling the smooth skin above her pert nose. "Then who'll be teaching the children?"

Seth gave her a nudge that sent her tripping across the threshold. "I will."

Roxey took that bit of information and considered it a moment. The father teaching the children? She hadn't run across this situation in the nine months she'd held this job. Was there a rule against it? She hoped so, then she wouldn't have to deal with this oaf of a man a minute longer.

She was startled by the gruff voice behind her. "Have a seat, and I'll get the kids."

She watched his back as he strode down a hallway and through a swinging door.

Well, the nerve! Sit where? She glanced around the entry hall. Not a chair in sight. The man's rudeness outweighed his bulk. While searching for a place to sit, Roxey caught her reflection in a mirror and let out a small gasp. She hurried to the oak coat tree in the hall and stretched up on her toes to get a glimpse of her face in its beveled mirror. Her hair was a tangled mess, and her face was smeared with a mixture of sweat and dust. She sank back down on her heels. What an impression she must have made!

She pulled a compact and a tissue from her purse and began to rub at the smudges, smearing them even more. The hinges on the swinging door squeaked, and she glanced up in time to see Seth Dandridge's head and chest appear around the door.

He pointed to a spot behind Roxey. "There's a bathroom through there. Help yourself." He disappeared again, the door flapping twice behind him before coming to a stop.

Roxey stuck out her tongue. He didn't see the childish display of temper, but it certainly made her feel better. In a huff, Roxey stomped off to the bathroom and tidied up the best she could.

When she emerged from the bathroom, she wandered into the living room to await the arrival of the "kids." *Goats have kids. People have children.* Roxey heaved a sigh and shook her head in exasperation. Another indication that Seth Dandridge was unqualified to teach anyone or anything.

The room she entered held simple furnishings. A sofa, two wingback chairs and a coffee table. They were excellent pieces and tastefully arranged. Yet something was lacking. Roxey turned in a slow circle. There were no pictures on the walls, no personal items lying around to give the room personality. Nothing. The room was as unsophisticated as the man who lived in it.

She chose one of the wingback chairs to sit in and pulled her briefcase onto her lap. While flipping through her files, she heard footsteps coming up the hall.

Her lips curved into a welcoming smile as two children appeared in the doorway. Both had obviously been spruced up for this interview. A young boy stood just in front of Mr. Dandridge, his eyes riveted on his boots and his hands shoved deep in the pockets of his jeans. His damp hair lay in furrows from the comb that had obviously just run through it. Like his father, he wore faded jeans, a blue cotton work shirt and boots. Unlike his father, he couldn't seem to look Roxey in the eye.

Beside the boy stood a small girl proudly bearing a tray of cookies. Roxey glanced at the open file in her lap and noted the child's name. Clarissa. What a beautiful name, Roxey thought, but such a big one for such a small girl.

The child's hair was brushed until it shone like spun gold, and an almost straight part creased the top of her head. Neatly tucked into the waist of her jeans was a light cotton blouse of pastel stripes, boasting a Peter Pan collar and puffed sleeves. Her blouse and the pink sneakers on her feet were the only things distinguishing her clothing from those of her brother. Unlike the other two, Clarissa offered Roxey a smile.

Seth placed a huge hand on his son's shoulder. "This is my son, Brandon." He raised his other hand to muss the top of the little girl's head. "And my daughter, Clarissa. Kids, this is Mrs. Classen."

"*Miss* Classen," Roxey corrected before smiling at first one, then the other. "It's nice to meet you, Brandon and Clarissa."

Seth prodded Clarissa. "Don't you have something for Miss Classen, Cissy?"

Cissy's sneakers squeaked on the hardwood floor as she hurried to Roxey's side. "I baked some peanut butter cookies specially for you." Her face beamed with pride as she held the tray out to Roxey.

"My, don't they look delicious!" Roxey took a cookie and a napkin from the tray. "Thank you, Clarissa."

"You can call me Cissy. Everybody does." Cissy set the tray on the coffee table and perched herself on the edge of the sofa, her hands squeezed between her knees, waiting for Roxey to take a bite.

How could such a bear of a man produce such an adorable child? The thought reminded Roxey of the presence of Mr. Dandridge. She turned to him and Brandon, who still stood in the doorway. "Why don't you gentlemen join us?"

"I…uh…" Seth stammered and stuttered, trying to think up an excuse to avoid this tea party. "I forgot the lemonade. I'll be right back."

"That's okay, Dad. I'll get it." Brandon charged around his father and beat it for the kitchen before Seth had a chance to stop him. Roxey watched Mr. Dandridge's face color as he shuffled into the room and sat in the chair opposite her, dwarfing it with his massive size.

She placed her napkin and half-eaten cookie on the table, then retrieved the Dandridge file from her lap. "Why don't we get started." She didn't ask it as a question, but as a statement of purpose. She was as anxious to end this interview as Seth Dandridge was to get her off his land.

Roxey was all business as she faced Mr. Dandridge. "Why do you wish to teach your children at home?"

If there had been room in the chair, Seth would have squirmed under Roxey's probing look. "Because I think I can teach them more than they're learning in public school."

"Are you a certified teacher, Mr. Dandridge?"

"No." Seth's gaze shifted from Roxey to Cissy, sitting on the couch, then to his knees, where he plucked at the dark line in the crease of his faded jeans.

"Then what makes you feel qualified to teach your children, Mr. Dandridge?" Roxey knew she was being blunt and much too callous, but she wanted out of this house...and wouldn't mind taking with her Seth Dandridge's apology for wasting her time.

He lifted his head and pierced her with his dark eyes. "Who says I'm not?"

Roxey flinched as if he had struck her. "Uh...no one. I just need to determine what qualifies you to—"

Brandon's entrance with the lemonade interrupted her. He approached his father's chair and held out the tray. Seth shook his head and nodded toward Roxey.

She took a glass and wrapped both hands around it. Condensation from the glass dripped onto the papers in her lap, and Roxey blotted at them with the heel of her hand before she took a sip of the tart drink.

"Brandon, you and Cissy get a bucket and go pick some blackberries."

Roxey nearly choked on her lemonade. Why was he sending the children away? She hadn't talked to them yet. She glanced at the forms and the unanswered questions, then at Seth.

He didn't say a word until he heard the back door slam. Then he turned to face her, his elbows propped on his knees and his hands clasped in one tight fist, his index fingers leveled at her like the barrel of a sawed-off shotgun. "I know my children and their needs better than you or anybody else in the school system. I don't need to prove to some prissy little city girl with a degree that I can teach." Seth stood, towering over her.

Each word he spoke slammed into Roxey with the force of a sledgehammer. She met his menacing glare eye for eye, and without moving her gaze from his she slapped the papers back into her case and slammed the lid down. "Fine, Mr. Dandridge. You'll receive my report by mail."

She made it all the way to the front door before she remembered her car was still stuck in the ditch. With an impatient groan, she wheeled around and immediately flattened her nose against the chest of Seth Dandridge. He gripped her shoulders to steady her while she unconsciously pushed against his chest. The tingles started again. From his chest, through her fingertips, and up her arm. She couldn't explain the sensation and didn't want to.

But Seth could. He felt it, too. And he was experienced enough to recognize it for what it was. Lust. Physical attraction. Desire. He could pin a hundred labels on it, but they all boiled down to the same thing. He was attracted to Roxanne Classen—in spite of the fact she represented everything he despised.

Roxey reached up and pushed his hands from her shoulders. "I need to use your phone to call a wrecker."

"Why?" His mouth curled up on one side in a lopsided smile, causing a dimple to wink at her from beneath his beard. She hadn't noticed the dimples before, but then he hadn't smiled before, which made her realize he was probably laughing at her.

"Because my car is in the ditch about two miles up the road." Roxey's eyes sparked with anger as she tightened her grip on the straps of her shoulder bag. "*Now* may I use the phone?"

He folded his arms, and tucked his chin to his chest as he looked down at her. "We don't have one."

"You don't have one?" Roxey's shoulders sagged in defeat. "I should've known. Anyone who would choose to live in this godforsaken place wouldn't want a phone. So how am I supposed to get back to town?"

"Sounds like a personal problem to me, lady." Seth turned and walked toward the screen door.

He hadn't taken two steps before Roxey stopped him with a firm grip on his forearm. He paused and looked down at her manicured hand, then at her. She dropped her hand to her side and grabbed a fistful of her silk dress. If she didn't hold on to something, she would be tempted to slap that smug look off his face.

"I agree it's my problem, but I came here at your request. So that makes it your problem, too."

Seth calmly stepped around her and moved to stare out the screen door, pulling at his beard as if deep in thought. "Maybe."

"Maybe *what*?" Roxey demanded in frustration.

"Maybe it's my problem, too," he replied slowly.

Roxey grabbed him by the elbow and pulled him around to face her. "You are a rude, overgrown, slow-minded—" she sucked in air through tight lips as she tried to think of a word insulting enough to call him "—mule!"

A mule, huh? He hadn't matched wits with a woman in a long time and there was something about arguing with this one that made his blood heat up. She looked as if she wanted to slap his face, and all he could think about was kissing hers.

"I have a tractor."

Roxey waited impatiently for him to say more. When he didn't, she said, "So?"

"If someone were to ask real nice, I might be willing to hook it up to her car and pull it out of that ditch."

Roxey sucked in a deep breath and blew it out through her teeth. A macho man. Just what she needed to end this wretched day. Now he was going to make her beg before he would agree to help her.

With her fists clenched at her sides, Roxey did something she'd never done before. She swallowed her pride. "Mr. Dandridge," she said, fighting for control, "will you *please* get your tractor and pull my car out of the ditch?"

With an irritating slowness, he turned and pushed the screen door open, then stopped and looked back over his shoulder at Roxey. "Why don't you have a seat. It might take a 'slow-minded mule' like me a while to figure out how to get that car out of the ditch."

Before Roxey could reply, the screen door banged shut behind him.

Two

For a moment, Roxey stood and stared wide-eyed at the empty doorway. Why, that ill-mannered oaf! If he thought she would stay one more minute in this house, he was crazy. She grabbed her briefcase and pushed through the screen door, letting it slam behind her. Even if she had to walk every step of the way to town, she wouldn't wait for him to help her. She marched down the stone path leading to the road, her chin held high. She would show him! Roxanne Classen had always managed to solve her problems, and certainly without ever being indebted to the likes of Seth Dandridge.

When she reached the road, she glanced back to see if he was in sight. He wasn't. He probably didn't even intend to help her, she thought irritably. More than likely he was off somewhere having a good laugh at her expense.

At the sound of an approaching engine, Roxey wheeled around. A truck was headed toward her. She knew it couldn't be Mr. Dandridge, because the truck was coming from the opposite direction. Running to stand in the middle of the road, Roxey waved her arm, forcing the oncoming truck to stop in front of her.

A wizened farmer leaned his head out of the truck's window. "Need some help, little lady?"

A deep sigh of relief escaped Roxey. "Yes. My car is in the ditch about two miles up the road. Could you help me pull it out?"

"Sure thing. Got a tow chain in the back." He pushed open the passenger door. "Hop in, but mind the dust. It's pretty thick."

In the barn, Seth stuffed a worn pair of work gloves into his back pocket, chuckling at his success in having the last word with Roxanne Classen. A slow-minded mule, huh? He laughed again as he pulled a heavy tow chain from the wall by the door.

A barn cat wrapped its body around Seth's leg, a deep purr rumbling deep in its chest. Seth stopped and rubbed the cat's ears. He planned on taking his good, easy time getting back to the house. It wouldn't hurt the little spitfire to cool her heels a while, he thought smugly.

Minutes later as he rounded the corner at the front of the house, Seth heard a door slam. He glanced in the direction of the road and saw old Jubal Henry's truck chug off down the road. Through the passenger window he caught a flash of red hair before the truck made the curve and disappeared from view.

Why, that little—With a last scathing look, Seth wheeled around, mumbling curses on one Roxanne Classen.

Roxey flew through the office with the force of a tornado. She swung her briefcase up and clapped it down on her gunmetal-gray desk with a deafening whack, drawing the attention of everyone in the room. After flopping down onto her swivel chair, she spread out her swollen feet in front of her in an unladylike sprawl. She kicked off her shoes and frowned at the dirt-filled cracks on the supple snakeskin, then rolled one shoe over with her toe to study the broken heel. Deciding they were probably ruined anyway, she scooped them up and pitched them into the metal waste-basket beside her desk.

"Damn that man!"

LaVerne Higgenbotham raised her head. "What did you say?"

Roxey wheeled her chair up closer to her desk and started yanking papers out of her briefcase. "I said 'damn that man.'"

Without even looking, Roxey knew LaVerne was frowning in disapproval. She always did when someone did something she didn't approve of. With her lips drawn together like the strings on a purse, her silver hair pulled back in a tight bun, and those high-collared, prim dresses she always wore, LaVerne looked like a dried-up old maid. But of course no one in the office dared call her one to her face. For thirty-two years she'd worked for the state. Her office was her home and the people who worked there her children. She clucked after them like an old mother hen and prided herself in knowing them better than they knew themselves.

LaVerne had grown accustomed to Roxey's sudden and unorthodox outbursts but didn't sanction cursing in her office from anyone—no matter whose daughter she was. "And whom, may I ask, are you damning?"

Roxey spun her chair until she faced her typewriter, her lips set in a determined line as she rolled the Department of Public Education, State of Kentucky letterhead around the carriage.

"Seth Dandridge."

Unable to contain her curiosity, LaVerne walked to Roxey's government-issue desk, perched her hip on the side of it and pulled her bifocals farther down her nose as she looked over Roxey's shoulder to see what she was typing. "Wasn't it the Dandridge family you interviewed today?"

"Yes. And believe me, it's the last time I'll drive out to no-man's-land to interview anybody. They can damn well come to the office." Roxey's fingers fairly flew over the keys as she beat out her frustrations on them.

LaVerne's nostrils thinned, and her spine stiffened. "Roxanne, I'd appreciate your refraining from using profanity in this office."

Roxey slumped over her typewriter, her face cradled in the crook of her elbow, the keyboard muffling her voice. "I'm sorry, LaVerne. It's just been a horrible day." She lifted her head, pinched the bridge of her nose between her thumb and index finger and fought back the tears burning the back of her eyes.

LaVerne bent to pat Roxey's tangled curls with a thin-skinned, blue-veined hand. "There, there," she soothed. "Let's go to the conference room and have a glass of tea, and you can tell me all about your horrible day."

She pulled Roxey up by the hand and led her to the conference room. After setting a glass of lime tea—LaVerne's cure for everything—in front of Roxey, the older woman pulled up a metal folding chair next to her. "Now tell me what happened."

Roxey took a sip, then backhanded the moisture from her mouth in a gesture unbefitting a woman of her breeding. Anger built as she thought again of her disastrous afternoon. "That damn man."

LaVerne's thin shoulders sagged in frustration. "Do you realize what you're saying when you damn someone?" Without waiting for a response, she continued her lecture. "You're putting a curse on him. Condemning him to hell. Now does Mr. Dandridge really deserve that?"

"I'm not sure *hell* deserves the likes of Seth Dandridge." Roxey pushed to her feet and paced around the small room. "He is rude, inconsiderate and mule-headed. And I'll be da—" She caught herself before completing the curse. She certainly didn't want to end up in hell with Seth Dandridge! "—darned if I'll give him permission to shut up those poor children on that farm and allow *him* to teach them."

LaVerne pressed her shoulders against the back of the chair and folded her hands primly in her lap. "Maybe you'd better tell me the whole story."

Roxey did— Beginning with her air conditioner quitting, including the rabbit darting out of the weeds, through her walk down that hot, dusty, insect-infested road, and ending with her appeal for help with her car.

"And if a farmer hadn't stopped and pulled my car back on the road with his truck, I'm sure Mr. Dandridge would have let me walk all the way back to town." Roxey sank onto her chair and drained her glass of tea, then rested her chin on her crossed arms on the tabletop.

LaVerne pressed an index finger to pursed lips, then cocked her head to look at Roxey's bent figure. "If you think Seth Dandridge should be denied the right to teach his children at home, then send him a letter of denial. But you better make sure you're basing your decision on more than the man's personality. It's his commitment and his ability to teach his children we're to evaluate, not his disposition."

"I know that. But he ended our interview before I could make any kind of assessment. I have no choice but to deny his request based on inconclusive information."

"Then be prepared for a fight. It doesn't sound as if he'll take your denial in stride." With a tug on Roxey's earlobe, she said, "Now enough of this nonsense. We've got another thirty minutes before we can call it a day."

Roxey plodded back to her desk in her stocking feet. She typed the letter of denial based on the inconclusive interview with Seth Dandridge, dropped it in the outgoing mail basket and promptly dismissed him from her mind. It was Friday afternoon, and the weekend stretched invitingly before her. From the bottom drawer of her desk, she pulled a pair of black leather flats and slipped them on. For the first time, she was tempted to forget her father's challenge, the job with the state department, and get on with her life.

But Monday morning found Roxey back at her desk, and at noon she packed her briefcase with the files for the interviews scheduled for that afternoon. A shadow fell across her desk, blocking out the fluorescent light glaring down from tubes encased on the ceiling. Glancing up, she saw a broad, blue-shirted chest. She lifted her gaze higher until it rested on the angry face of Seth Dandridge.

Not again!

He slapped a letter down on her desk with his broad hand splayed on top of it. Grease lined his fingernails. "Just what exactly is this supposed to mean?"

Determined not to be intimidated by his anger or his size, Roxey pried the sheet of paper from beneath his hand with her thumb and index finger. With a forced calm, she scanned the letter.

And they say the postal service is slow!

She cocked her head and looked up at him. "This is the report from our interview, as I'm sure you're aware."

With both palms flattened on her desk top, he leaned until his face was only inches from Roxey's. The pungent odor of grease and the sweet smell of freshly mown hay assailed her.

"Why the denial?"

Roxey finished packing her briefcase and snapped it closed. "Surely you aren't surprised? After all, you ended our interview, Mr. Dandridge, not I."

"Then how do you know I'm not qualified to teach my kids?"

"In the first place, they aren't 'kids,' they're children. Secondly, you didn't give me the opportunity to determine otherwise."

Seth pushed off her desk and wheeled to glare out the window, then back to face her again, his hands cupped at his hips. "Okay, so interview me now. I've got the time."

Roxey stood and slipped her purse strap over her shoulder. Clutching the handle of her briefcase in her hand, she gave him a polite smile. "Sorry, Mr. Dandridge, but I don't." And with a toss of her head she turned and walked away.

He caught her by the elbow as she rounded the desk, but when she gave his hand a scathing look, he abruptly dropped it.

With her chin and nose in the air, Roxey weaved her way through the office, ignoring the curious looks she received from her fellow workers. But when she reached her car, Seth was there one step ahead of her. She tried to step around him, but with each move he blocked her path.

Roxey dropped her briefcase with an impatient thump. "Now what?"

"Give me five minutes. That's all I ask."

She turned her wrist and glanced at the face of her Rolex. "Okay, five minutes. Start talking."

Seth jammed his fists at his hips and twisted his upper body away from her, then whipped back, his voice tight with anger. "You have got to be the stubbornest woman I've ever met."

When she reached for her briefcase, his fingers circled her wrist. Hunkered down in front of her, he lifted his head until his gaze met hers, their faces only inches apart. "I want to teach my kids at home. Is that a crime?"

With him at such close proximity, Roxey was forced to meet his gaze. Hours of squinting in the sun had left wrinkles fanning the corners of his eyes and had bleached the tips of his eyelashes a deep gold. His eyes were intense, pleading, and in them Roxey saw the same desperation she heard in his voice. More than the strong fingers cinched at her wrist, it was that desperation that held her captive, forcing her to hear him out.

"They're a darned sight better off on the farm with me than they are in school. I know their needs, and I'm willing to give them the time they need to learn at their own level."

At the mention of the farm, Roxey remembered again the isolation of the Dandridges' home, and a ridiculous picture of the children laboring in the fields beside their father played across her mind. "Mr. Dandridge, based on the information available my answer is no and will continue to be no. Those children cannot learn anything working on a farm. They need to be in school." She realized she was viewing the situation in black and white terms, but was so exasperated by him she no longer cared. She twisted free from his grasp. "Now, if you'll excuse me."

He stepped in front of her. "Give me one week."

She closed her eyes and sucked in a deep breath, then opened her eyes to glare at him. "Will you *please* get out of my way?"

Ignoring him, she slipped the key into the door lock, but before she had a chance to turn it, Seth reached down and pulled the key from her grasp.

"Just one week. Stay on the farm with us for one week, and I swear I'll prove to you I can do it."

She snatched the key back from him and turned to insert it again. With a quick twist, she unlocked the door, and swiftly opened it before he had a chance to stop her. One hand gripping the door, she turned and offered him what she hoped was a placating smile. "Mr. Dandridge, I'm sure your intentions are admirable, but I do not make it a policy to conduct overnight interviews with any of my clients. Now, if you'll excuse me." Roxey stepped around the car door.

"The kids'll be there to chaperon. You don't need to worry yourself about that."

Roxey almost laughed. A chaperon? That was the least of her worries. "And suppose I agreed to give you the time, Mr. Dandridge. What if at the end of the week my answer were still no?"

Seth ducked his head and scraped his boot across loose gravel on the parking lot, his voice so low Roxey strained to hear. "Then I'll send 'em to school."

His acquiescence drew a frown to Roxey's face. Obviously, the man was serious if he was willing to gamble it all on her impression after only one week.

"What do you think my spending a week on your farm will prove?"

All signs of supplication disappeared from his face as he glanced up at her. He folded his arms across his chest and leaned his hip against the waxed finish of her car. "I think you've denied me permission because I'm a farmer."

Roxey started to interrupt, but he held out a hand to stop her. "And personally, I don't think you know enough about farm life to make that kind of decision."

His gaze traveled down the length of her, from the carefully styled hair to the Ralph Lauren dress, and on down to the soft leather of her Italian shoes. When the direction of his gaze cut to the hood ornament on her BMW, she became acutely aware of the difference in their life-styles. Ralph Lauren's sophisticated country look somehow seemed counterfeit when confronted with the reality of a farmer's grease-stained jeans and sweat-stained chambray shirt.

She quickly swallowed her denial. The man had her there. First of all, she knew absolutely nothing about life on a farm. And secondly, she admitted reluctantly, the farm *had been* the basis for her decision. That, of course, coupled with the fact that Seth Dandridge had in no way proved to her he was qualified to teach his children.

As was her habit when deep in thought, Roxey caught the soft skin of her lower lip between her teeth and frowned. There were the children to consider. Her priority in every case she handled was the welfare of the children. Home schooling might be just what the Dandridge children needed. She had no way of knowing; Seth had ended the interview before she'd made a true assessment. He'd also shown his stubbornness by only offering on his application the barest information about his family and leaving blank the questions regarding *why* he wanted to pursue home schooling.

And, too, the opportunity to actually see a home school in progress—something she rarely had the chance to experience—would certainly give her new insight into her job. In office meetings, the topic had been tossed around, but as yet none of her co-workers had investigated the possibility.

The idea of spending time on the Dandridges' farm began to appeal to Roxey. She had vacation time due her, though she'd planned to meet her friend Justine in the Bahamas. But she'd been to the Bahamas before. Roxey fought back a smile at the thought that a week watching Seth Dandridge struggle to change her mind might be more fun.

A scheme began to form in her mind. If she agreed to visit the farm, it would be only fair for the Dandridges in turn to visit her, and when they did, she would have the opportunity to show him what the children would be missing by being removed from public school and their friends.

No one else in her office would ever consider doing this, Roxey knew without even asking. But then Roxey Classen wasn't anyone else. She planned to do what she thought was right and worry about getting approval for it later.

"All right, Mr. Dandridge. I'll spend a week on your farm...but on one condition. You and the children have to spend a week in Louisville at my town house. If your intention is to prove the benefits of home school for your children, I'd like the opportunity to show you what they might be missing."

"But—"

"No buts, Mr. Dandridge." Roxey extended her hand. "Do we have a deal?"

Silence hung heavy between them before Seth reluctantly placed his hand in hers and slowly shook it. "Yeah, we got a deal. Come about noon Sunday."

The tingles started again. Through his palm, into hers, sending prickles of electricity shooting up her arm. Flustered by these strange sensations, Roxey snatched her hand from his and bent to retrieve her briefcase.

As she stepped to the car door, she cast a furtive glance in his direction. He'd already reached his dust-covered pickup and was climbing in. She watched as he folded his long body into the cab. He looked like a mountain man with that scraggly beard and too-long hair. But there was something about him...something that made her pulse quicken.

She tossed her briefcase onto the passenger seat and hurriedly slid behind the wheel, thinking maybe the chaperons weren't such a bad idea after all.

Oh, Lord! Why'd I do that? Seth hit the steering wheel with the heel of his hand. *A week with Roxanne Classen?* His anger dissolved as fast as cotton candy when he remembered Brandon and Cissy. They were worth it. If he had to entertain the whole damn Louisville Garden Club, they were worth it. His kids needed specialized instruction, and he intended to see they got it. He twisted the key in the ignition and revved the engine. With a grinding noise, he shifted into first gear, eased off the clutch and headed the truck for home.

He knew he was biting off a big responsibility. With the farm work, housework and caring for the kids, he already carried a full load. And now he was adding teaching them, as well. The hours he'd already spent reviewing textbooks and planning lessons were proof enough of the commitment home schooling required. But there was no other choice. He brushed a weary hand across his eyes and thought, if they only had a mother...then quickly discarded the thought. They *had* a mother. A selfish, disinterested, poor excuse for a mother, but a mother nonetheless.

There had been a time when Seth thought he had discovered Thoreau's Walden—a veritable utopia. For a while everything had gone as he'd planned. The move to the country, the completion of their log home, the clearing of the fields for pastureland and crops. Then the disappointments came, and with them Seth had become more and more cynical and had withdrawn to the farm, shutting out the world beyond.

With two young children to raise and a farm to manage, his days were filled. Seth had accepted the responsibility and for five years had never regretted his decision. Until now. No! he thought, gripping the steering wheel until his knuckles ached. He didn't regret it. But he needed help. School was the problem. If only his children didn't require special attention, he was sure the public school system would satisfy their needs. But what with Brandon *and* Cissy needing special encouragement, he had only one choice—to teach them himself at home.

By the time he reached the dirt road leading to the farm, he'd calmed down. The country always had that effect on him. The clean air blowing through the truck's open windows and the serenity of the landscape acted like a sedative, slowing him down and forcing him to appreciate his surroundings.

Dark furrowed fields and blue-green pastures dotted with grazing cattle edged the road on either side of him. Spring rains had gutted out the road, leaving deep tracks and even deeper potholes. A weary sigh slumped his shoulders. What with the planting and hay seasons, he hadn't had time to grade the road. With his gaze leveled in front of him, he noticed something he'd missed earlier on his trip to town. Tire marks cut into the hard-packed dirt before swerving off into the ditch.

Seth felt a pang of remorse. This must be where Miss Classen's car had slid off the road. He glanced at the tall pines two miles farther down the road that marked the site of his log home, and felt even worse. The woman had walked all that way in the hottest part of the day. No wonder she'd been in a bad mood. And because of his rudeness she'd been willing to walk back rather than wait for him to help her.

He stomped on the brake and twisted on the seat to glance back over his shoulder. Another set of tracks—wider than the tracks made by the tires of her car—cut across the road. Must be the tracks of old Jubal Henry's truck, he thought in shame. Not only had he allowed Roxey to leave without his help, he'd permitted old Jubal to do work Seth Dandridge himself should have done.

Seth twisted back around and rested his forehead against the top of the steering wheel. Guilt pierced his chest. No wonder the lady had turned him down flat. He'd treated her worse than he would an ant at a picnic.

He pushed off the steering wheel and hit it with a balled fist. *Why'd they have to send a spruced-up city girl like Roxanne Classen? Why couldn't they have sent some old lady to interview him?* That prissy little thing with those damn high-heeled shoes and that gaudy diamond ring. She should've stayed in the city where she belonged.

Then he remembered their deal. One week. He had one measly week to prove to her he could teach his kids. He sat up straighter in the cab and vowed to be on his best behavior. A cocky grin split across his face. Hell, that woman wouldn't even recognize him as the same man. He would be so nice and helpful, she would be more than happy to give him the permission he needed.

Then he remembered his promise to spend a week in Louisville, and the smile slowly faded. He didn't want to spend a week in the city. Who would do the farm work? Milk the cows, bale the hay, feed the chickens and weed the garden?

He stomped on the clutch and jerked the gearshift into first. *Humph. Just like a city girl. Thinks you can drop everything and run off and play.*

When his log home came into view, Seth saw Cissy and Brandon waiting for him out front. They ran to greet him as he stepped down from the truck.

"Hey kids! Y'all been good for Miss Bertha?" Seth scooped Cissy up and swung her up to ride on his shoulders. He walked toward the house with one arm draped across Brandon's shoulder and a hand clasping Cissy's knee.

"Yeah, we been good. Miss Bertha made us a blueberry pie for dessert, and me and Brandon got to bake the leftover crust into cinnamon crisp." Cissy bent over the top of her daddy's head and planted a kiss on his forehead. "And we saved you some."

"Well, thanks, Cissy." He patted her knee and bent to look at Brandon. "Did you remember to feed the chickens?"

Brandon scuffed along at his father's side with his hands stuffed deep in his pockets. "Yes, sir." Without lifting his gaze from the ground, he asked, "Did you talk to that lady again?"

Seth raised his hands to lift Cissy down as they reached the porch steps. He sat down on the third step and pulled

Cissy to his lap where she snuggled up against him, rubbing her cheek against his beard. "Yeah, I talked to her. She's coming next week to stay with us for a while."

Brandon jerked his head up, his eyes wide with alarm. "Why?"

"So she can decide if it's okay for me to teach you kids. We're going to have to be on our best behavior. We didn't make a very good impression last time."

Cissy's mouth puckered into a pout. "I wasn't bad. Shoot, I made peanut butter cookies and everything."

Seth threw back his head and roared with laughter. "No Cissy, it wasn't you. Daddy was the one who was bad."

Cissy gave his beard a tug. "Then you better be on *your* best behavior."

After her last interview Monday afternoon, Roxey headed her BMW for Louisville. She set the cruise control at fifty-five and relaxed, her right elbow on the leather armrest, and lightly holding the padded steering wheel with the fingertips of her left hand.

The afternoon's interviews had gone well, and she mentally affirmed her decision to approve the families for home teaching. Both the mothers she'd interviewed had presented Roxey with lesson plans, proposed field trips and projected goals.

Though there were those in the office—and out—who doubted Roxey's intentions, she was dedicated to her job. She was determined to ensure that the needs of the children were considered above those of their parents. And the two mothers she'd interviewed today had earned her approval and the right to teach their children at home.

Roxey rubbed her fingertips against her temple as the Dandridge family came to mind. Had she been unfair in denying them approval? No, she thought as she placed both hands on the steering wheel, locking her elbows and glaring at the road ahead. If a mistake had been made, it was Seth Dandridge's. He hadn't given her the opportunity to properly interview him . . . or his children. Anger at Seth Dandridge quickly dissipated as she focused her mind on the children.

Brandon. So quiet and serious. Standing by his father, he'd looked like a miniature version of Mr. Dandridge. Roxey rubbed her fingers across the smooth leather upholstery of her car. Why was the boy so shy? He hadn't even been able to look her square in the eye. So unlike his sister.

Cissy. Roxey smiled as she thought of her, sitting on that sofa with those big blue eyes and that almost-straight part in her hair. So proud of the cookies she'd baked for "Miss Classen." Roxey felt her smile tug higher. And those pink tennis shoes. Such a little lady in spite of her boyish clothes. Roxey had seen the pink polish smeared across the little girl's fingernails and knew it was the child's own attempt at femininity. How she would love to dress up Cissy in a frilly dress, and tie up those beautiful curls with ribbons, allowing the child the opportunity to fully express her ladylike yearnings.

Roxey frowned at her own thoughts, her shoulders drooping in resignation. She knew it was silly to think like that. Her job was to approve or disapprove the family for home teaching. Period. The children's mother should be the one worrying about them.

Where *was* their mother, anyway. Was she deceased or were she and Mr. Dandridge divorced? Roxey mulled that over for a moment, then decided the woman must be dead. After all, what judge in his right mind would give a man like Seth Dandridge custody of two small children?

She flicked on her directional signal and took the Louisville exit. But her thoughts remained on the Dandridge family.

What in the world would LaVerne say when they discussed Roxey's plans for her vacation? Roxey laughed out loud. She knew her supervisor would see the merit of the idea, but she also knew she would worry. While Roxey and Seth stood in the parking lot arguing, Roxey had seen LaVerne peeking through the venetian blinds that covered the office window. At the slightest sign of distress on her part, Roxey knew without a shadow of doubt LaVerne would've called the police and had Seth Dandridge locked up.

Roxey sobered at the thought. Was Mr. Dandridge a violent man? She quickly dismissed the thought. No. Just rude.

She pushed the button for her garage door opener and drove under its protective covering. After turning off the ignition, she slumped back against the leather-upholstered seat. A week in the Dandridges' home. How would she ever be able to stand a whole week living under the same roof with that mule of a man?

Three

Roxey jogged up the front steps of the Dandridges' log cabin with her garment bag slung over her shoulder and her makeup case in her hand. She dropped the case at her feet and pounded the screen door with the heel of her hand while shifting the weight of the hanging bag to a more comfortable position. The sound of her knock echoed through the silent house. She waited a moment, then visored her face with her hands and peered through the screen. No one appeared to be home.

She looked around the yard. Again, nothing. Glancing at her watch, she replayed their conversation in her mind. He had said Sunday noon, hadn't he? She walked to the side of the porch and leaned over the cedar rail to peer behind the house at the barn. Cupping her hands at her mouth, she called, "Hello-o-o-o!"

Cissy appeared at the barn door, jumping up and down and motioning for Roxey to join her.

After tossing her bags on the porch, Roxey ran down the steps and along the path leading to the barn. When she stepped between the wide double doors of the massive structure, she stopped for a moment, letting her eyes adjust to the sudden darkness. Cissy slipped her small hand into hers.

"Shhh," Cissy whispered. "The baby's sleeping." She tugged on Roxey's hand, then quickly dropped it when they reached an open stall door.

Roxey took a tentative step and peered inside. Mr. Dandridge knelt on the hay, while Cissy and Brandon stood pressed against his shoulders. Their backs were to Roxey and they were all looking at . . . something.

Curious, Roxey stepped behind Cissy and looked over the top of Mr. Dandridge's head. A calf lay on the hay, its sides heaving as it fought for each breath.

Without ever acknowledging her presence, Seth answered her unasked question. "We found him this morning. His mama died."

"Will it live?" Roxey asked in a soft whisper.

"Maybe. We'll have to bottle-feed him." Cissy and Brandon stepped back as Mr. Dandridge stood and turned to face Roxey. "How'd you like to take care of him?"

Roxey pressed three fingertips to her chest. "Me? I don't know anything about calves."

"Don't have to. You just have to feed him."

Roxey swallowed hard, then lowered her gaze to the calf. It looked so pitiful lying there on the hay. "If you're sure I can handle it . . ."

Seth bent down and scooped up the calf. "First thing we have to do is get him to stand up. It's important for him to move around to clear his lungs." He supported the calf as he attempted to stand on wobbly legs. "Brandon, get the calf formula out of the storeroom. Cissy, you get the calf bucket. Miss Classen, run up to the house and bring us a big pan of warm water."

"Roxey."

Seth stopped and turned to her, a puzzled look on his face. "What?"

"Roxey. My name's Roxey."

He frowned at her, then turned his attention back to the calf.

The children didn't hesitate. They headed in different directions to do his bidding. Not to be outdone, Roxey ran to the house. She jerked open cabinet doors in the unfamiliar kitchen until she found a large pan. After filling it with hot water from the tap, she jogged back to the barn, water sloshing over the sides of the pan and running down her fingers.

Winded, she thrust the pan at Seth and stepped back, pressing her palm against a stitch of pain in her side. The calf stood on wobbly legs at Seth's side. On the floor of the barn at Cissy's feet sat a bucket with a long nipple sticking out its side. Brandon held a bag in his hands.

"Cissy, measure out one and a half cups of the powdered milk. Brandon, we need three pints of water. How many cups are in a pint?"

"Two."

"So how many cups of water do we need?"

"Six."

"How many ounces to a cup?"

"Eight."

"So how many ounces will we need?"

"Forty-eight."

Brandon responded to all four questions before Roxey had figured out the first. The questions sounded like story problems from her elementary math books. What was Seth Dandridge doing, trying to impress her with his teaching skills already? She glanced at him through narrowed eyes, but found him intent on stirring the milky mixture in the bucket.

He hit the spoon twice on the side of the metal bucket, startling Roxey, then turned and held out the bucket to her. "Give it a try."

After wiping sweaty palms on the seat of her cotton slacks, she reached for the bucket. Her fingers brushed his as they made the exchange, his sure and strong, hers trembly. She took two slow steps toward the calf and stuck out the bucket. The calf didn't move. Roxey turned uncertain eyes to Seth. "Now what?"

"You got to make him think it's his mama. Rub some of the milk on the nipple and talk to him."

Roxey dipped her fingers in the warm milk, then, wrinkling her nose in distaste, rubbed the sticky liquid around the nipple. Hesitantly, she stepped closer to the calf and nudged his black nose with the nipple. "Come on, baby, drink your dinner."

The calf licked at the nipple, then with a gentle tug, began to suck. An excited smile lit Roxey's face. "She's doing it!"

"He."

Roxey looked over her shoulder and frowned at Seth. "He? How can you tell?"

Cissy giggled, Brandon rolled his eyes and Seth flushed beet-red. He pointed underneath the calf's belly. "The plumbing."

Roxey held the bucket with both hands and leaned over to peek under the calf. She laughed without embarrassment at her obvious mistake. "Oh, I see."

The calf gave the bucket a greedy tug and Roxey nearly lost her grip on it. With a laugh, she pulled the nipple from the calf's mouth. "Sorry, little fellow. All gone." She knelt down in front of him and rubbed his velvety nose. "You need a name, don't you, fellow?"

Seth folded his arms across his chest and snorted in disgust. Just like a city girl. Thinks you have to put a name on everything. "How about T-Bone or Sirloin?"

Clapping her hands over the calf's ears, Roxey glared over her shoulder at Seth. "Not in front of the baby. Please." She motioned for Cissy. "Come here, Cissy. You and I will name him." Giving her hair a haughty toss, Roxey showed Seth her back as she slipped an arm around Cissy's slim shoulders. "What do you think, Cissy? A name's awfully important."

Cissy rubbed her hand across the blaze of white on the calf's face. "I like Baby Calf, Miss Classen."

Roxey suppressed a smile. How original! "Baby Calf it is then."

Seth's voice, heavy with sarcasm, came from behind them. "If you two are through with the christening, we'll go down to the creek for a swim."

"Whoopee!" Brandon threw his cap up in the air, caught it, then sailed out the door with Cissy right behind him, the newborn calf forgotten in their excitement.

"Give me the bucket, and I'll wash it out. Did you bring a swimsuit?" Seth closed the stall door and hooked the wire loop over the top post.

"Yes. Where do you want me to change?"

"At the house. Upstairs. Second door on the right. Cissy'll show you." Without another word, he turned and walked to the back of the barn, leaving Roxey alone at the barn door.

"And welcome to you, too, Captain Friendly," she grumbled as she followed the path back to the house.

After reclaiming her bags from the front porch, Roxey climbed the stairs in search of her room. The door on the left was closed, but the door on the right stood half open. She peeked through the opening. A white iron bed with a white eyelet comforter and dust ruffle dominated the room. Matching drapes slowly swayed at the open windows on either side of the bed. A tennis shoe lay on the pink, heart-shaped rug spread on the wood floor. About a foot to the left lay the other shoe. Roxey nudged the door open farther and followed the path of discarded clothes to the bathroom door. "Cissy?"

"In here," came a muffled voice.

Cissy stood in the middle of the bathroom floor with her T-shirt and arms stretched above her head, her face covered by the shirt.

"I'm stuck."

Roxey dropped her bags and sank to her knees in front of Cissy. "Here. Let me help." With a quick tug, she pulled the shirt over Cissy's head, then held out the swimsuit for the little girl to step into. After tying the straps at her shoulders, Roxey said, "Now how about showing me my room?"

"Yours is right through there." Cissy pointed at the opposite door. "We share a bath." She skipped to the door and flung it wide. "You going swimming with us?"

Roxey picked up her bags and followed. "You bet I am."

"You afraid of snakes?"

Roxey's face paled and her bags slumped from lifeless fingers to the floor. "Snakes? D-did you say snakes?"

A breeze whispered through the branches of the tall oaks lining the banks of the creek, offering a cool respite from the July afternoon heat. Clumps of grass clung to the steep slope leading to the edge of the water. Above the creek the limb of a giant oak stretched out over the water, and from it swung a weathered rope with a huge knot tied at the end. Roxey's eyes were riveted on the dark water below the knot. *You afraid of snakes? You afraid of snakes?* Cissy's question played through her mind over and over again. Despite the heat, a shiver shook Roxey's shoulders.

From behind her, Cissy's and Brandon's voices carried above the sound of the running creek, as they argued over who got to swing first.

Seth firmly silenced their bickering. "Miss Classen gets to go first. She's our guest."

Roxey wheeled to face Seth, her eyes wide in her pale face. "No. That's okay, really." She pulled a quilt from the bag they'd packed and busily began to spread it. "I think I'll just relax and watch, if that's okay. And please call me Roxey."

"Whatever makes you happy. Okay, kids, let's flip to see who gets to go first." He pulled a quarter from the pocket of his cutoffs and flipped it, then caught it in the fist of his right hand. He slapped the coin to the back of his left. "Call it, Cissy."

"Heads."

He lifted his hand to expose the coin. "Heads it is. You first, Cissy. Brandon, you get the rope."

Grudgingly, Brandon shinnied up the tree and inched out across the limb. With his stomach pressed against the limb's rough bark, he swung the rope back and forth in ever-increasing arcs until Seth's fingers grasped it.

Roxey sat perched on the quilt with her knees pulled beneath her chin, her stomach somersaulting as she watched Cissy climb up the slope in preparation for the first swing into the creek. Cissy took two running steps then drew her knees up before swinging out over the water. Roxey watched Cissy arc to the far bank, then drift back toward the middle of the creek. Something moved in the water to the left of Cissy, and Roxey focused on the long, dark shape gliding through the water. She squeezed her eyes shut when she heard the splash as the little girl hit the water. *Snakes. Oh, God! They'll be all over Cissy.* Without thinking, Roxey bolted for the bank of the creek, pulling her shirt over her head as she ran. She plunged into the cool water, high-stepping until the water reached the top of her thighs, then swam. She reached the spot where Cissy had disappeared just as the child's blond head surfaced. Hooking her arm around Cissy's neck in what she hoped was a lifesaving maneuver, Roxey pulled the struggling child to shore.

Seth met them there.

"What in Sam Hill do you think you're doing?" he shouted as he pulled the sputtering Cissy from Roxey's arm. "She knows how to swim."

Roxey's breath came in deep gasps. "S-snakes. A-afraid they'd g-get her." She dropped to her hands and knees, mud oozing up between her fingers and around her knees. Weak. She felt so weak.

"Snakes!" Seth shouted above her. "What snakes? There aren't any snakes out here."

Roxey's head lolled between her elbows, her breath labored from a combination of effort and nerves. She pushed back to sit on her heels, dragging her muddy palms along her thighs. "I saw one." She lifted a hand and pointed at a spot near the bank. "There."

Seth walked to the edge of the bank and fished out a stick. "You mean this?"

Realizing her mistake, Roxey offered helplessly, "Cissy asked if I was afraid of snakes. And when I saw that . . ."

Seth shifted his gaze from Roxey down to Cissy, who stood dripping at his side. "You know there aren't any snakes out here, Cissy. Why'd you tell Miss Classen that?"

Cissy's lower lip trembled. "But Mama never swims with us 'cause she's afraid of snakes. I just asked Miss Classen if she was, too."

Brandon stood off to the side watching the proceedings in silence. Cissy, tears now rolling down her cheeks, looked up at her father. Seth scowled down at her, his hands splayed on his hips.

And Roxey laughed. It started with a low chuckle, then grew to a full-blown howl as she bent double, pressing her stomach with mud-smeared hands.

Three pairs of eyes turned to her. She tried to stop laughing, but she couldn't. The absurdity of her trying to save Cissy from the snakes was just too much.

She batted a weak hand at the others, then doubled over again. "I—I'm sorry," she gasped. "It's just so funny! *Me* saving Cissy from the snakes!"

Seth watched Roxey struggle to her feet. She was crazy. She had to be. Nobody in their right mind carried on like this. His gaze traveled from her sodden hair, down her mud-splattered body to her bare feet, then back up. She might be crazy, but damn, she was stacked!

From the spandex straps at her shoulders to the elastic circling high on her thighs, the one-piece bathing suit hugged her petite figure. Everything in between was curved, flat or ripe. Seth blew out a long breath and shuddered. It had been a long time since he'd seen a woman in a swimsuit. Too long, judging by the sudden swell in his cut-off jeans.

Impatience sharpened his voice when he turned to his son. "Brandon, get the rope. It's your turn."

While Brandon shinnied back up the tree, Roxey—still laughing—walked to the edge of the water and crouched down. She splashed water over her arms, thighs and knees, washing away as much of the gray-brown mud as possible.

Seth stood three feet away, waiting for Brandon to swing the rope to him. He glanced down just as Roxey tilted back her head to splash water at her neck. The deep V of her cleavage winked back at him, her breasts pushing at the skimpy material cupping them. His breath whooshed out of him in a low whistle.

Roxey glanced up at him, then followed his gaze to her breasts. She placed a tentative hand there, then looked back at him, the smile slowly fading from her lips. His eyes burned into her. Roxey felt the heat three feet away.

From above them, Brandon yelled, "Watch out, Dad!" But the warning came too late. The water-logged knot of the rope slapped against the side of Seth's head, knocking him off balance. His arms flailed the air as he rocked first backward then forward, struggling to regain his equilibrium. It soon became obvious he would lose the battle, and Roxey watched water shoot five feet in the air as Seth belly flopped into the creek.

Roxey paced back and forth across the length of the guest room. Everyone else had gone to bed more than an hour ago, but she wasn't sleepy. Each time she closed her eyes, her mind played back in Technicolor the events of the wild afternoon. She pressed the flat of her hand against the crisp silk at her chest...the skin beneath the fabric still burned from the intensity of Seth Dandridge's gaze.

She walked to the window and pushed back the curtain, allowing the moonlight to flood the room. The yard below was bathed in shadows, and from somewhere way off she heard the bawl of a cow. A cool breeze blew across her face, teasing her with the heady scent of pine and magnolias.

Wide-awake and restless, she grabbed a silk robe and pulled it on as she tiptoed down the hall and stairs. At the front door, she paused and glanced back over her shoulder in the direction of Seth's bedroom. His door was closed, and no light showed beneath it. Careful not to make any sound, she held the front door with one hand while slowly pulling with her other. With only a slight creak of the hinges, she eased the door open and slipped out to the inky blackness of the porch.

The moon drew her to the railing, where she stopped and looked up at the night. Stars sprinkled the dark sky like diamonds on a canvas of blue-black velvet. Nothing at all like her view from the city. Everything here seemed sharper, brighter, closer. Roxey hugged her arms under her breasts, closed her eyes and breathed deeply of the night air. Scents of pine and magnolia blended with those of freshly cut grass and honeysuckle. It was glorious!

She tossed back her head and threw her arms wide as if to encompass it all. There was something peaceful about this place. Cleansing. Even freeing.

"Couldn't sleep?" Seth's voice came from below, startling Roxey. He perched a boot on the bottom step, leaned his weight on his forearms crossed at his thigh and looked up at the woman he'd invited to spend a week on his farm. The moon spotlighted Roxey, bathing her in its silvery beam, and giving her skin an ethereal glow. Her hair picked up its light and blazed with rich flames despite the silvery shine. She looked like an angel and a gypsy all rolled into one. Seth couldn't take his eyes off her.

Roxey hugged one arm at her waist, and pulled at the neck of her robe, embarrassed to be caught traipsing around in her nightgown. If she'd known he was still up, she would have slipped on her jeans and shirt before coming downstairs.

With the moon behind Seth, she could see only his silhouette, his face shadowed and indistinct. "No. I usually don't go to bed this early."

No, I bet you don't, Seth thought irritably. Her evenings probably began about the time his ended. He envisioned her partying till the wee hours of the morning with her jet-set friends, drinking and dancing and carrying on. Seth glanced back over his shoulder at the moon and the pastoral setting of his farm, and thought how dull all this must seem in comparison.

While his head was turned away from her, Roxey studied his profile in the light of the moon. The wide forehead, the slope of his straight nose, the mustache partially covering his lips and the swell of his muscled chest. Goose bumps popped out on her arms. She took in a deep breath and slowly exhaled it, trying to slow her suddenly racing pulse.

He turned to her, his face falling again into shadow. Silence stretched heavy between them and Roxey racked her brain for something to say to fill the awkward void.

"Cissy didn't mean to scare me."

"I know."

"She's such an intelligent child. I'll bet her teachers have a hard time keeping her occupied."

Seth pushed off his knees and turned to sit on the bottom step, his back to Roxey. "No. In fact, the opposite's true." He plucked a leaf from a shrub beside the steps and began to shred it. "Cissy has trouble reading. She went almost the whole school year before they tested her and found out what was wrong. They say she's dyslexic. The other kids make fun of her because she can't read."

Roxey moved down the steps and sat beside him, thrilled at the opportunity to discuss the children's needs. "Is that why you want to teach her at home?"

"Yes."

"What about Brandon? Wouldn't it be easier if you sent him to school so you'd have more time for Cissy?"

Seth tossed the shredded leaf to the ground and rested his forearms across his thighs, his shoulders slumping under the weight of his problems. "No. Brandon's got the opposite problem. He's too sharp. School's boring for him. He catches on to everything real quick and whips through his assignments. But his teacher says he's a troublemaker. Hell, the kid's bored. He doesn't have anything else to do, so he gets into trouble."

With her arms wrapped around her legs, Roxey propped her chin on her knees and studied the polish on her toenails. Seth's application for home teaching began to take on a new perspective. Now, especially, she wished he had taken the time to explain his reasons and the children's needs. His request no longer appeared selfish. In fact, it was quite the opposite. But whatever his reasons, Roxey still wasn't convinced.

"Just because they have special needs doesn't mean you have to teach them at home. There's a special school in Louisville for children with dyslexia and private schools that might challenge Brandon more." When Seth didn't respond, she cocked her head to look at him. "Have you checked into any of them?"

"No."

"Why not?"

An owl hooted, its call lonely and haunting in the darkness. Seth stood and stretched, then turned to look at Roxey. All week long he'd thought about her. Half the time worrying she wouldn't come and the other half worrying she would. At the oddest times he'd found himself thinking of her. Of that wild mane of hair and those eyes as clear a blue as a summer sky. Right now her forehead was wrinkled up with deep lines and he regretted he was the cause of them. He held out his hand to her, palm up. "Would you like to swing?"

Roxey hesitated. She didn't want to swing. She wanted to continue their conversation. And she wanted him to answer her question. But his outstretched hand pulled at her like a magnet. Saving the questions for another time, she stood, petite beside his massive frame, and placed her hand in his. With her arm tucked beneath his, he led her across the yard, the dew on the grass cool beneath her bare feet, dampening the hem of her robe.

Beneath the branches of the magnolia tree, Seth released Roxey's arm. He stepped behind the swing and gripped its ropes, steadying it while Roxey settled onto the weathered board.

"I can't remember the last time I did this," she said nervously as she wrapped her fingers beneath his on the bristled rope and pushed off with her toes.

"Me, either." Seth's hands caught her waist and pulled her back, back, then flattened against her spine as he shoved her forward.

Roxey soared toward the branches overhead, brushing the lowest leaves with the tips of her toes. One full arc was all it took before memories of childhood games she'd played on her swing set filled her mind. Sometimes she had pretended to be a famous trapeze artist preparing for her first leap, or an astronaut rocketing through space.

But none of her childhood memories matched this sensation. It was like flying, the moon her destination.

The wind caught the silk around her and billowed it out, exposing her legs to midthigh. She swung back and Seth's hands brushed against her waist, then were gone, leaving a yearning for his touch in their place. Back and forth she swung, higher and higher, until her head spun with the dizzying sensation.

She laughed and the wind picked up the melody of her laughter and filled the air with its music. Leaning back against the ropes, Roxey let her head fall back, allowing her hair to flow free and wild behind her while she pointed her toes at the three-quarter moon. Blood rushed to her head, warming her cheeks and leaving her giddy.

Her laughter drew a smile from Seth as he watched her strain to touch her toes to the dark, shiny leaves. Moments ago she'd been all business, quizzing him about his children. Now she was sailing through the air, chasing the wind through the tree.

Moonlight, filtered through the magnolia's dense foliage, played across Roxey's uplifted face. Her cheeks were flushed and her eyes bright with excitement as she swung away from him, teasing him with her laughter.

Earlier—when she'd stood on the porch bathed in moonlight—he'd thought her an angel or a gypsy. Now he was sure she was a wood nymph, who had come to enchant him with her laughter. Mesmerized by the innocence of her beauty and her lack of inhibition, when the swing arced back toward him, Seth caught the ropes above her hands and pulled himself up, placing a foot on either side of her hips. The branch overhead creaked under the burden of his added weight. He bent down, and holding on to the rope with one hand, he circled Roxey's waist with the other. Easing her up, he eased down, until he sat on the swing and Roxey on his lap.

The shock of being lifted then dropped onto Seth's lap had Roxey clinging to the coarse ropes. Sure she would fall, she scooted back, molding her body to Seth's. His body felt warm and solid against hers, the muscles in his legs and stomach taut as he worked to pump the swing higher.

The sensation was not an unpleasant one, which in itself surprised Roxey. She allowed her head to drift back against his shoulder, and her emotions to run free. It seemed only natural to release her hold on the rope and to cling instead to the arm at her waist as they soared through the air. His beard brushed against her face, tickling it softly. She glanced up over her shoulder at him, and in the moonlight a dimple peeked at her from beneath his reddish-brown beard. Roxey returned his smile.

Up close, Seth's eyes didn't seem quite so forbidding. In fact, the warmth of his gaze seeped deep within her, making her vividly aware of the intimate fit of her body to his. She remembered the tingles she'd felt before at his touch and decided they were nothing compared to the shock waves racing through her now. She wondered what it would be like to feel his lips on hers. Quickly stifling her wandering thoughts, she looked away from his penetrating gaze.

Small clouds of dust rose at their feet as Seth dragged his boots across the hard-packed dirt. The swing slowed, then gradually stopped. He released his hold on the rope and slipped his arm to Roxey's waist.

A soft wind blew tendrils of her hair across his face. With a work-roughened hand he brushed it back, then rested his cheek against her hair, breathing deeply to fill his senses with the essence of her. She smelled of coconuts and soap and flowery feminine things. It had been a long time since he'd held a woman in his arms. He closed his eyes and drank in the sensation, picturing Roxey as she had looked that afternoon in her bathing suit, all curvy and ripe. A need long denied burned within him, and he tightened his hold on her.

The moon, the stars, the heady scent of the faded magnolia blossoms all worked at Roxey's emotions, robbing her of common sense and propriety. When she felt his arm tighten at her waist, she turned in his arms until her lips were only a whisper away from his.

His gaze bored into hers—demanding, denying. One kiss. Just one kiss. What would it hurt? A niggling doubt made her hesitate. She knew her purpose in spending a week with the Dandridges was to rule on their application for home schooling. But she also knew that her decision—despite the sensations Seth was arousing in her at the moment—would not be influenced by her emotions. She would make the right decision for the children, one not shadowed by her feelings for their father.

With this resolved in her mind, she gave herself up to the moment. In slow motion, Seth's face drifted closer until his lips brushed hers. His mustache and beard feathered across her mouth and chin, then chafed lightly as he deepened the kiss.

His kiss—nothing like his appearance—was polished, sophisticated . . . seductive. His lips moved over hers, his touch as soft as that of the breeze lifting the leaves above them. Yet it was as if a whirlwind had caught her, whipping up sensations she'd never experienced before.

From her waist he smoothed his hands upward across the slick silk of her robe, gliding over her, barely touching, leaving shivers of excitement in his wake as he made a slow journey to the gentle curve of her throat. His fingers splayed from jawline to shoulder while he lifted her chin with his thumbs, tilting her face up to meet his, demanding more.

While gently drawing her bottom lip between his, he slid his thumbs down the smooth column of her neck to the hollow of her throat, moving the balls of his thumbs in slow, burning circles against her velvet skin. He stopped abruptly when his fingers tangled in the necklace at her throat, and Roxey winced as the diamond drop dug into her flesh.

Seth felt the wince against his lips and withdrew to see what was caught in his fingers. A diamond the size of a large pea winked at him in the moonlight.

Diamonds. The sight brought home exactly whom he held in his arms. Damn! What had come over him? With an oath he jumped up, in his haste dumping Roxey on the grass at his feet.

When she hit the ground, Roxey's teeth snapped together with a loud click. For a moment she was too stunned to move—but not to speak. "You big oaf! What'd you do that for?"

His chest heaved as he fought for calm. This woman represented everything he detested: wealth, society, city life. And besides all that, she was here to judge him, and he desperately needed her approval. Angry at himself for his lack of control, his voice was sharp when he spoke. "I'm sorry. I shouldn't have done that."

She stood and dusted off her robe with quick, angry jerks of her hands. "Sorry for what? Kissing me or dumping me on the ground?"

"Both."

"Wrong," she said as she gathered up the tails of her nightgown and robe in tight fists. She stood to face him, her chin high in angry defiance. "The kissing was fine. Dumping was the mistake." She spun on her heel and stomped to the house, ignoring the pebbles that cut into her bare feet.

Seth stood under the sprawling limbs of the magnolia and watched her flounce to the house. When the screen door banged shut behind her, he slammed his fist into the tree trunk, the rough bark cutting into his knuckles. Damn her! Why did she affect him this way? He'd lived the life of a monk for five years and had been perfectly content until she appeared in his life. Why now? And for God's sake, why her?

Four

Be still now, Trixie, while I help you put on your pajamas."

The sound of Cissy's voice drifted through the closed door. With her hairbrush poised in midstroke, Roxey frowned at her reflection in the bathroom mirror. *Trixie? Who's Trixie?* After two full days on the Dandridges' farm, Roxey was sure she'd met everyone, including every barn cat and stray dog within miles of the place. She pulled the brush through her hair and cocked her head toward the door separating the bathroom from Cissy's room. Cissy's voice drifted through again.

"Me and Miss Classen had so much fun today. She helped me gather the eggs after breakfast and helped me weed the garden. Then we went for a walk down by the creek and picked wildflowers."

Roxey laid her brush on the counter top and pressed the heels of her palms against the cool tiles as she realized Cissy was talking to an imaginary friend. Without making a sound, Roxey tiptoed to the door and listened.

"Miss Classen showed me how to arrange them in a jar and we put them on the kitchen table. Daddy acted like he thought they were silly, but I think he really liked 'em. He likes Miss Classen, too. I can tell."

Roxey's mouth sagged open. Like her? The poor misguided child. The man despised her!

"Wouldn't it be neat if Miss Classen and Daddy got married? Then she could live with us and we could have fun all the time."

Roxey clapped a hand over her mouth to stifle a gasp. Guilt for listening in on the private conversation warmed her cheeks. Before she heard anything else not meant for her ears, she quickly knocked on the door, then pushed it open. Cissy sat in the middle of the bed struggling to put pajamas on a sculptured doll.

"Hi, Cissy. Who's your friend?"

"Trixie Gail. I adopted her. I have papers and everything."

Roxey sat down on the side of the bed and took the doll Cissy offered her. She smoothed the yarn hair then finished snapping the pajamas. "She's very pretty. Do you talk to her a lot?"

Cissy took the doll back and hugged her to her chest. "Oh, yes. I tell Trixie Gail everything. She knows every secret I know. But it's okay, 'cause she can't talk."

Roxey laughed and ruffled Cissy's hair. "That's the best kind of friend to have. Isn't it time for you to be in bed?"

"Yes, ma'am, but I had to dress Trixie Gail, and sometimes she just won't be still long enough for me to get her pajamas on her." Cissy scooted to the head of the bed and slipped under the covers, tucking the doll in beside her and flashing Roxey a smile. "You can kiss me good-night if you want to."

A slow warmth crept through Roxey, making her eyes bright as she bent down and pulled the covers up to Cissy's chin before placing a kiss on the child's forehead. "Good night, Cissy."

As Roxey turned to leave, Cissy called out to her. "You forgot to kiss Trixie Gail."

Roxey moved back to the bed and leaned over and kissed the cool plastic of the doll's face. "Good night, Trixie Gail."

While Roxey was bent over the bed kissing the doll, Cissy reached up and circled Roxey's neck, bringing with her scents of lemon and talcum powder. Roxey closed her eyes and hugged the freshly scrubbed child to her, all the while trying to swallow the lump of emotion building in her throat. "'Night, Miss Classen."

"'Night, Cissy."

Roxey quickly crossed the room and pulled the door behind her, then sagged back against it, biting her lower lip to stop its quivering. That precious little child. So much love to give and no one but a doll to lavish it on. She needed friends. Real friends. The kind who talk and tell secrets, too.

Roxey sucked in a shuddery breath and squared her shoulders. It was time to have a talk with Mr. Seth Dandridge. She marched down the stairs and through the darkened hall to his office. A triangular patch of light shone onto the hall's oak floor from the partially opened door.

"Seth?"

Roxey pushed her fingertips against the smooth wood panels and called again as she peeked through the widened opening. "Seth?" The chair behind the mahogany desk stood empty, and there was no sign of its occupant anywhere.

Roxey tiptoed into the room for a better look. *So this is where he hides.* She turned in a slow circle, surprised at the room's furnishings. Darkly stained furniture and a leather couch with framed hunting prints hanging above it dominated the small room. Bookshelves covered the wall to the left of the desk. She stepped closer to examine their contents. Leather-bound copies of classics by Thoreau, Dickens, Twain, and even Shakespeare shared space with textbooks on farming and ranch management. Books on gardening and seed catalogs were propped up with a football trophy.

Intrigued by this glimpse into a side of Seth Dandridge she'd never seen, Roxey moved behind the desk to study the framed certificates on the wall. A diploma caught her eye. She quickly skimmed over the smaller print to read the bold letters: University of Kentucky, Bachelor of Science in Biology, Seth A. Dandridge. Her gaze flew to a second diploma. University of Kentucky, Master of Business Administration, Seth A. Dandridge.

What? Part of Roxey's brain warred with what her eyes told her was true. But how? Why! He certainly didn't *look* like a man with two college degrees, nor did he act like one.

She quickly glanced at the contents of the other frames. Above the diplomas hung a picture of the University of Kentucky football team. She stood on tiptoe for a closer look at number 64. My God! It couldn't be. But it was! Seth Dandridge glared down at her from the back row of the team's picture. Dressed in a football uniform with his helmet tucked under his arm and with black smudges beneath his eyes, he appeared even bigger and meaner than when Roxey had first seen him standing on his front porch.

She took a step to the right and found herself at eye level with a picture of a beardless Seth standing with one arm looped around a beautiful woman's shoulder. A baby lay sleeping in the crook of his other arm. He didn't look like the same man. With his hair cut short, and without the beard, he looked almost...well, almost handsome. And the smile. *Smile?* Roxey snorted and leaned in for a closer look. After all, it was the first one she'd seen up close and in the daylight. She was curious. Deep dimples pierced each cheek while wrinkles fanned the corners of his eyes.

"What are you doing in here?"

She jumped at the sound of Seth's voice, but when she turned to him, she covered her embarrassment with a cool and composed expression. "Looking for you."

He stepped into the room and closed the door behind him. "You found me. So what do you want?"

Roxey propped her hip against the desk and with a flip of her hand gestured to the wall behind her. "You can start by explaining all of this."

He looked at the wall, then away. "There's nothing to explain."

"Oh, yes, there is. Why didn't you tell me you graduated from college?"

Seth moved to the bookcase, plucked a book from the shelf and began to thumb through it. "What difference does it make?"

"Plenty!"

With a loud "humph," Seth slammed the book closed, replaced it and reached for another. "A piece of paper does not make a man, but a man can make a piece of paper."

"Confucius? Or is that pearl of wisdom a Seth Dandridge original?"

He glanced up long enough to frown at her, then returned his attention to the book.

Roxey refused to permit him to ignore her. "Why do you allow people to think you're just a dumb old farmer?"

He looked up again, this time with one eyebrow arched at her. "'Just a dumb old farmer?' I know a lot of fine men who'd take offence at that statement."

"You're right. I'm sorry. Let me rephrase that. Why do you allow people to think you're dumb?"

"I really don't care what people think of me."

"Why?"

"Why should I?"

"Well…" Roxey grasped for a reason but came up empty. "Because."

"'Because'?" Seth laughed. "And you worry about people thinking *I'm* dumb?"

Roxey frowned. She knew she was losing ground but refused to admit defeat. She slid off the desk and moved to face the diplomas, tapping her nail against the glass. "Why didn't you use your degrees?"

"Who says I didn't?"

Roxey wheeled to face him, her face tight with anger. "You are the most infuriating man. I'm only trying to better understand you and your family, and you're doing everything in your power to aggravate me."

Her anger surprised him, yet he knew what she said was true. He'd invited her here for just that purpose—to get to know him and his family so she could see for herself how his kids would benefit from home schooling.

Without moving his gaze from her face, Seth closed the book and pushed it back into the stack. "I did use my degree. I worked for nine years for a company based in Louisville." He pointed to the plaques displayed in the bookcase on the wall beside him. "For three years running, I was their number-one salesman. They promoted me to management, and for two years my district led the nation in sales. Then they promoted me again. This time to the home office. I was their golden boy. Vice president and on my way up the ladder."

Roxey watched his eyes narrow and his lips thin to a tight line barely visible beneath the mustache and beard as he glared at the reminders of his past.

"Then what are you doing here on this farm?"

He slowly turned his head until his dark eyes met her blue ones. "I'm here because I *choose* to be."

Undaunted by his clipped answer, Roxey pressed on. "But why?"

Seth walked over to her and leaned to place a hand on the desk top on either side of her. With her buttocks pressed tight against the desk and his body looming over her, Roxey was trapped.

"Do you have any idea what corporations do?" He leaned closer until she felt his breath blowing warm and moist against her face. "They eat people alive. They're like a huge vampire. They suck the life's blood out of you, then when they're through with you, they cast you aside."

Watching Seth as he spoke was like watching a storm brew. Emotion swirled and built on his face like thunderheads in a turbulent sky. With each word he uttered his eyes became darker and more intense, and he leaned closer and closer until Roxey was bent back over the desk as far as she could go. With one hand pressed against the desk for support, she pushed the other against his chest to stop him.

"Seth. Please. You're hurting me." She felt his heart pounding against her hand as she watched the veins pulse in his neck.

For a moment he stared at her as if only just realizing her presence. He ducked his head, his forehead brushing lightly against hers, and sucked in a deep shuddery breath before pushing away from her. With his back turned to her, he mumbled, "I'm sorry. I didn't mean to hurt you."

Roxey stepped behind him and touched her fingertips to his back. He flinched. "It's okay." She slipped her hand into his as she stepped around to peer up at him. "Why don't we sit down and talk?"

Without waiting for his response she led him to the leather couch. Tucking her feet underneath her, she sat down and propped her elbow on the back of the couch, and her cheek on her palm. "Not all corporations are vampires, Seth."

He arched a brow at her. "Oh? And what do you know about corporations?"

"My master's thesis was on corporate theory."

Seth laughed, but his laugh lacked humor. "Life isn't always like what you find in books."

"Then you tell me what corporations are like."

"Numbers. A pyramid of numbers." At first his words were slow and deliberate, but gradually his voice rose and the words poured out of him like a raging river whose waters had flooded its banks.

He jumped up and began to pace. "It's like living in a pressure keg. Always worrying about profits and budgets. But never the people behind the numbers."

"If you hated it so much, why did you stay?"

"Because it wasn't always like that. In the beginning it was a challenge. I loved my job. I set goals for myself, achieved them, then set higher ones.

"Everything was going great until we were caught in an economic decline. In order to save the company, expenses were reduced. More than a hundred people were laid off. Good people who depended on their jobs to put food on the table. Then buy-outs were offered to people close to retirement."

"But if the company was having financial difficulties, they didn't have a choice."

"They had a choice, all right. They could have decreased stock earnings and cut some fat off the salaries of management. Mine included."

A frown deepened on Roxey's face as she watched him pace back and forth in front of her. "Did you suggest that?"

He stopped in front of his desk and leaned back against it as he plowed his fingers through his hair. "Oh, yes. They let me know real quick that I, too, was expendable. That's how the game's played. The unwritten rules of success in the fast lane. You pull down anybody who stands in your way. If the budget's too high, you start looking for ways to cut. It's the law of nature—the weak and the old go first."

With his hands pressed against the desk top, he cocked his head to look at her. "One morning I woke up and looked at myself in the mirror. What I saw made me sick. All I could think about was all the people who had lost their jobs. And I still had mine. It was a sobering realization. By accepting the company's methods, I was sacrificing my own beliefs. I decided then and there that I was getting out while I still had a little self-respect. I bought the farm and moved my family out here."

Silence hung heavy between them while Roxey assimilated this knowledge. This was the longest and most enlightening conversation she'd had with Seth Dandridge. Yet there was so much more she needed to know, things she didn't have the answers for. "Where is Mrs. Dandridge?"

"Louisville. She hated the farm. Said it was smothering her. She packed up and left."

"You mean she willingly left the children with you?"

"Yes."

"Why?"

"Baggage. *Excess* baggage, to be exact. Lorissa enjoyed the life-style we had while I worked for the corporation. After six months here on the farm, she decided she'd had enough and moved back to the city. She knew she couldn't support herself and the children and continue the social life she craved. So she left them with me. She sees them occasionally. At her discretion."

Noticing the look of shock on Roxey's face, Seth asked, "Why does that surprise you?"

"It's just hard to imagine a mother walking away from her own children. Cissy couldn't have been more than a year old."

"The key word there is *mother*. Lorissa was never a mother. When she left, Cissy was eighteen months old and Brandon was almost six."

"How do you manage? I mean with the farm work, the housework and the children? Do your parents help?"

"My parents have been dead for almost eighteen years. They were killed in a car wreck when I was a freshman in college. As far as managing, well, I wouldn't be if it weren't for Miss Bertha." He picked up a paperweight from his desk and began to toss it back and forth between his hands. "Her husband used to work for the same company I did. He was one of the ones who was offered a buy-out. Nine months after he retired, he died. When I went by after the funeral to see Miss Bertha, she told me that after he retired, he just gave up. She said that without his job, he lost his sense of purpose and direction. He just didn't seem to have a reason to live anymore."

Seth caught the marble weight in his right hand and squeezed until his knuckles turned white, ridding himself of the anger these memories brought. He stared unblinking at the paperweight in his hand, then set it down on the desk, a deep sigh escaping him. "It was about that same time I decided to move out here. Ed and Miss Bertha never had children, so Miss Bertha was all alone after he died. The whole time we were moving I couldn't get her off my mind. Somehow I felt responsible for her welfare. So I made a deal with her. If she'd move out here with us and help with the kids, I'd build her a house and she could live here for the rest of her life. She'd always loved Cissy and Brandon and she's a country girl from way back, so she jumped at the chance. We'd been doing just fine until this school thing came up.''

Roxey's chest felt as if it was on fire. Realizing she'd unconsciously been holding her breath, she released it with a soft whoosh. All of her initial judgments about Seth Dandridge were going up in smoke. Uneducated? Hardly. Dumb? Only an act. Heartless? No way. Who was Seth Dandridge? Definitely a much more complex man than she had first given him credit for being.

Maternal instincts she didn't know she possessed surfaced. She had a sudden yearning to wrap her arms around him and pull him to her breast. She wanted to make up for all the bad things in life he'd experienced. Mentally shaking herself, she slowly rose from the sofa. He hadn't asked for her pity, and she knew without asking he would never accept it.

His reference to the problem with school and the children reminded her of why she'd come to his office in the first place and helped her broach the subject of Cissy's imaginary friend. ''That reminds me. While I was getting ready for bed, I heard Cissy in her room talking to herself.''

''Not to herself. To Trixie Gail.''

Roxey's eyes widened in surprise. ''You know?''

''If you mean do I know Cissy talks to her doll, yes.''

''I don't think that's healthy.''

With his tongue tucked into his cheek, Seth chuckled softly. ''Come on, Miss Classen, surely you had an imaginary friend when you were growing up?''

Roxey's chest swelled and her chin lifted in a defiant stance. Yes, she'd had a friend. An imaginary friend. One that she loved and talked to because there hadn't been anyone else there for her. But that wasn't any of his concern.

But it was why she wanted so desperately to see that Cissy had a *real* friend to share her love with.

"Yes, but that isn't the point. Her doll is all Cissy has. She needs playmates."

"She has Brandon."

"I mean little girls. Her own age. Someone she can share her secrets and her dreams with."

Seth folded his arms across his broad chest as a smug smile settled on his face. "And just what makes you an authority on little children, Miss Classen? How many have *you* raised?"

She snapped her head around to face him. "You don't have to be a parent to see when a child is lonely, Mr. Dandridge."

Seth stood to tower over her. "And you think Cissy is lonely?"

The fact that she had to look up a good foot and a half to meet his gaze didn't intimidate Roxey. "Yes, I think she's lonely. I think you're being selfish by insisting on teaching her at home and removing her only opportunity to be with children her own age."

"I told you why I need to teach her here."

"No, you told me why she couldn't function in a public classroom. You haven't explained to me why she can't go to a private school. If it's the money—"

"My financial condition is no business of yours."

"I didn't imply that it was. I was only going to mention that scholarships are available for those who need them."

Seth walked around the desk and sat down. He pulled out a thick ledger and a stack of invoices and began to pencil entries into the ledger. "If you'll excuse me, Miss Classen, I have work to do."

There was one personality trait Roxey had witnessed on their first visit and subsequently throughout her stay as a guest in his home that he hadn't managed to change her opinion of. He was still as stubborn as a mule!

She might be from the city, but she knew enough about mules to know sometimes it took a two-by-four between the eyes to get one's attention. With this in mind, she flattened her palms on his desk top and leaned over until her face was only inches from his . . . and waited.

He ignored her.

Roxey leaned closer.

With an impatient sniff, Seth bent farther over his books and continued to pencil entries onto the ledger sheet. The sniff proved to be a mistake. It filled his head with the scent of her perfume. Irritated, he glanced up, his gaze centered on the graceful curve of her throat. The V of her cotton sweater drew his eyes lower to the swell of her breasts. He swallowed hard and forced his gaze higher. A mischievous glint sparked her blue eyes as they met his.

"I thought we agreed you'd call me Roxey?"

"I—" A frog caught in his voice. He cleared it and started again. "Yes, we did." His face flushed a crimson red before he bent his head over his ledger again. "If you'll excuse me, I've got some bookkeeping that needs my attention."

Roxey slowly straightened and folded her arms beneath her breasts, forcing them to thrust upward against the ribbed fabric. I'll bet it does. A smug smile tugged at her lips as she watched the lead snap on his pencil. She turned and strolled slowly to the door. Wiggling two fingers at him, she said, "Good night, Seth."

Without looking up, he yanked open his desk drawer to search for another pencil as he mumbled, "Good night."

When the door clicked closed behind her, Seth slammed the drawer shut and reared back in his chair, slapping a palm to the desk. "Damn that woman!"

Everything about her was wrong for him. She was too young, too rich, too sure of herself. He jumped up from his chair and started pacing across the narrow space behind his desk. Then why did he want her? He clapped his hands down on the back of his chair and dropped his head between his elbows. He filled his lungs with slow, deep breaths. It didn't help. His loins still burned with the memory of the sun-kissed skin valleying between her breasts.

He pushed off the chair and wheeled to face the framed photographs behind his desk. His gaze focused on the one of him and Lorissa taken at Brandon's christening. With that coal-black hair, porcelain skin and sultry smile, it was no wonder he'd fallen in love with Lorissa Bodean. If only he'd looked deeper, he would have seen how superficial her beauty was. His ex-wife had been too young, too rich, a spoiled brat who refused to grow up. A whole lot like Miss Roxanne Classen. The confrontation with his past served to cure what the deep breaths hadn't. With a frustrated sigh, he sat back down and picked up his pencil. He'd have to be more careful around Miss Cla—Roxey, he quickly amended before reaching for the stack of invoices again.

What an unforgivable thing to do! Roxey pressed the flat of her hands against her hot cheeks as she hurried up the stairs to her room. Never in her life had she stooped to such low measures! Flaunting her body like some cheap floozy. Honestly!

A slight shiver shook her shoulders as she entered her room and walked toward the bathroom. Monica would have done to Seth Dandridge what Roxey had just done and more. That was what hurt…the fact that she had acted just like her older sister. For years, Roxey had watched Monica use her feminine wiles to get what she wanted from men, and it was because of this that Roxey had determined to use her mind, *never* her body.

She turned on the tap and splashed cold water on her face to cool her flushed cheeks. Using the towel beside the sink, she patted her face dry. The vanity mirror reflected her flushed face and, as she removed the towel from her neck, the amount of bare skin revealed at the V of her sweater. She leaned over and felt the heat rise in her face again as the fabric fell away from her breasts, exposing the deep valley between the rounded fullness of her breasts. What a cheap ploy she'd used to get his attention! She straightened and lifted her chin at her reflection. Well, she couldn't erase what had just taken place in Seth's office, but she could darn well make sure it never happened again!

Five

———

The following day Roxey found it easy to implement her vow. Seth avoided her like the plague. If she entered a room, he exited it. Unless the children were present. Then he would direct his attention to them and ignore Roxey completely.

Tense from the silent war being waged against her, that night after everyone was in bed, Roxey slipped out the back door and hurried to the barn, seeking solace in the one place she knew her presence was welcomed.

Roxey put her hand over her nose and mouth to block the foul odor that greeted her. She inched her way through the blackness, feeling her way through the darkened barn as she crept to the stall where Baby Calf was penned. Moonlight—cast through tiny square windows high above her—illuminated rectangular patches on the narrow walkway between the two rows of stalls.

Something furry brushed against her bare leg and Roxey stifled a scream as she leaped back, flattening herself against the wall. She flicked on her flashlight and with shaky hands played the light around the floor until its beam rested on a barn cat. Feeling a little foolish and a whole lot like what Cissy would call a fraidy-cat, Roxey turned off the light and pocketed it. She slipped the wire off the post and pulled the stall door open. The fresh hay she and Cissy had spread for the calf that morning was covered with manure.

"Baby Calf? You okay?" she whispered as she eased over to him. She frowned when the calf didn't move. He had grown so accustomed to her and the bucket that he usually met her at the gate. She knelt down and reached out a tentative hand to his face. Her finger brushed against his nose. It was cold and dry. Fear churned in her stomach and slipped its icy fingers around her throat, cutting off her breath. She moved her hand to his side. It, too, was cold and hard. She jerked her hand back and clutched it at her waist. Hot tears burned behind her eyes. No! He couldn't be dead. She'd done everything Seth had told her, hadn't she?

Her shoulders shook, and she sunk her teeth into her lower lip to fight back the tears. *He's just cold. He needs a blanket to warm him.*

She wiped at her nose with the back of her sleeve as she stood and backed out of the stall. Denying what she knew to be true, she walked to the tack room, pulled out a horse blanket and carried it back to the stall. Her eyes burned hot and dry as she spread the blanket over the calf.

From the tool rack on the wall she pulled a rake and with quick angry jerks she cleaned out the stall, careful not to disturb the calf. When she finished, she climbed the ladder to the loft. It took every ounce of her strength to push and shove a bale of hay to the loft's edge and over to the floor below. In the storeroom where Seth kept his tools, she found a pair of pliers and snipped the baling wire off the squared hay. After pulling off a section, Roxey spread the fresh hay around Baby Calf, crooning soft comforting words to him as she worked.

Seth sat propped up in bed, reading a farm magazine. His reading glasses rode low on his nose and he glanced up over the top of them when he heard the back door creak open and then shut. He glanced at the alarm clock on the beside table. Ten o'clock. *Now where's she going this time of night?*

He shrugged and picked up the magazine again. Roxey was a big girl. If she wanted to go outside, who was he to stop her? He focused again on the article concerning artificial insemination of cattle, but read only a paragraph before his mind wandered again to Roxey.

He'd done everything possible to avoid being alone with her. It was easy during the day with the kids around, but at night after they were in bed was a different story. He had taken to closeting himself in his room with magazines and books to avoid being alone with her. But it didn't help. His mind always wandered back over the day's events, picturing her laughing with Cissy or working in the garden or playing with that damn calf. An enigma. That's what she was. Wearing those silk shirts and designer jeans while sashaying around the barnyard. Dipping those manicured, diamond-laden fingers into dirty dishwater. Spitting watermelon seeds off the back porch twenty minutes after correcting Brandon for putting his elbows on the table while he ate. Seth's stomach shook as he laughed. She was a puzzle all right.

He didn't realize how far his thoughts had carried him until he glanced over at the clock and realized it was almost eleven. Then he began to worry. He hadn't heard her return to the house. She was unfamiliar with the layout of the farm and as green as they came. For all he knew, she could be wandering around out there lost. That worrisome thought had him out of bed and pulling on his jeans and boots. He didn't take the time to find a shirt before charging out the back door in search of her.

When he didn't find her on the porch or in the yard, he decided more than likely she was with the calf. But when he entered the barn, he quickly decided he wouldn't find her there, either. The smell that greeted him almost choked him. Immediately he identified the odor. The calf was sick. Torn between the need to check on the calf and the equally pressing need to find Roxey, Seth promised himself to return to the barn and examine the calf as soon as he'd located Roxey.

He turned to search elsewhere, but something made him turn back. He played his flashlight in front of the stall door and caught sight of the bale of hay broken open and beside it the pile of dirty hay. They hadn't been there earlier when he had done the evening chores.

Curious, he followed the beam of light to the stall, where he found Roxey sitting on the floor with her back to the wall. In the glow of his flashlight, he saw that her eyes were closed and sprigs of hay clung to the delicate fabric of her blouse and to her hair. Softly he called her name.

At the sound of his voice, her eyes flew open, wide with fear and guilt. He glanced down at the calf whose head lay in Roxey's lap. Without examining it, he knew it was dead. Scours. He'd seen enough of the disease to recognize it right off. If an orphaned calf died, that was usually why. The disease was like dysentery. The calf just dehydrated and died.

Why was she sitting in this stinking stall with a dead calf? In two steps he crossed the length of the stall and knelt at Roxey's side. At closer inspection, he saw that her eyes were red and puffy, and tears streaked her face. A pang of guilt hit him hard in the chest. He should never have given her the calf to care for. From the beginning, he'd known the animal's chances of survival were slim, but he hadn't known how attached Roxey would become to it.

He pulled the blanket up over the calf's head then gently moved it from her lap. He eased down beside Roxey and wrapped an arm around her shoulder. A shudder racked her slim body. She covered her mouth with her hand to hold back the tears, but couldn't. They came in great heaving sobs that shook her small body.

Seth pulled her into his arms and held her, smoothing his hand down her wild mane of hair. With her face buried against the breadth of his chest, he felt the warmth of her tears as they streaked down her face and tunneled through the springy hair covering his bare chest. She felt so small and vulnerable wrapped in the circle of his arms. A need to protect her surfaced. He knew he had to get her out of the barn, away from the calf and the terrible stench.

He pulled her up with him as he stood, then scooped her up in his powerful arms and carried her from the barn. As he stepped through the door into the barnyard, he sucked in great gulps of fresh night air. When he reached the backyard, he felt he'd put enough distance between Roxey and the barn. He collapsed onto a glider and settled Roxey on his lap. Sobs continued to rack her, and Seth felt at a loss as how to comfort her.

With his foot pushing against the dew-laden ground, he held her, whispering soft words of comfort while the glider moved beneath them in a slow, hypnotic rhythm.

The glider's soothing motion and the security of Seth's arms calmed Roxey. Her sobs gradually slowed, changed to occasional hiccups, then, at last, stopped altogether.

Her voice quivered when she finally spoke. "He's dead, isn't he?"

"Yes." Seth felt another shudder pass through her body.

Roxey had never dealt with the death of an animal before. When her pets had become old or sick they'd always just disappeared, and a new one was bought to replace it.

"I killed him."

Her disparaging tone cut Seth to the quick. He hugged her tighter against his broad chest, wanting to take her guilt and pain and absorb it into himself. "No. It wasn't your fault. Calves have a hard time surviving if they don't have a chance to nurse before their mamas die. You did everything you could to help him live."

While in the barn, the chill of death had penetrated Roxey to the bone, but now the broad expanse of Seth's chest offered warmth and security, his arms a shelter, protecting her from it all. No man had ever held her like this or comforted her this way. Not even her father when, as a child, she was sick or hurt.

Unwilling to let go of this secure feeling, she nestled her head beneath his chin, allowing his beard to intertwine with her hair. One of her hands rested against the flat of his back, while the other lay pressed between her cheek and the tight springy hair of his chest. Her eyes drifted closed and the gentle sway of the swing soothed her.

The even rhythm of Roxey's breathing told Seth she was asleep. With great care, he rose to his feet and carried her into the house and up the stairs. As he shifted her weight in his arms to fumble with the knob to her bedroom door, Roxey roused slightly, wrapped her arms around his neck and nuzzled her nose against his bearded chin. He swallowed back a wad of emotion that threatened to choke him as he gazed down into the beauty and sleepy innocence of her tear-streaked face.

A door opened behind him, and Seth turned to find his son standing in the hallway. Anger mottled Brandon's face, and his lower lip quivered, threatening tears, but before Seth had the opportunity to offer an explanation, Brandon wheeled into his room and slammed his door behind him. Seth started to follow him, then remembered he still held Roxey in his arms. With a cursory glance, he saw that her denim skirt had ridden up above her knees, exposing bare, shapely legs. He sucked in a deep breath and released it with a whispered oath. How could such a small woman cause so damn much trouble?

Steam billowed from the pot of grapes boiling on the stove, filling the kitchen with a sweet, tangy smell. Jars lined the counter tops like soldiers going to war, while baskets of grapes sat idle on the floor.

Miss Bertha flapped around stirring this, tasting that, and bossing everyone around. "Everyone" included Roxey and Cissy—Seth and Brandon had managed to escape to the woodpile out back. It appeared that making jelly was woman's work and the men were exempt.

Roxey scanned the room, making note of all the pots, pans, bowls, fruit and utensils lying about. "Wouldn't it be easier to buy jelly at the grocery store?"

Miss Bertha wheeled around and placed her hands on her ample hips. "Heavens, yes!" She winked at Roxey. "But it just doesn't taste the same. You'll see. Cissy, go out to the porch and bring me that box of jar lids by the back door. Mind you don't spill any. Roxey, you come here and stir these grapes."

The wooden spoon traveled from Miss Bertha's age-freckled hand to Roxey's smooth, manicured one, and Roxey began to stir. From her position at the stove, Roxey could see Seth and Brandon at the woodpile. Two-and-a-half-foot sections of logs were stacked four feet high and ten feet long, waiting to be split. Seth stood beside the stump of a long-dead tree, resting his weight on an ax as he talked to Brandon.

She was impressed again at how mature the children were and how industrious. There wasn't a lazy bone in either of their bodies. She wondered if that was inborn or trained and shook her head. From her experiences with her cousins' children, she decided it must be trained, and her relatives needed a new trainer because she'd never seen them lift a finger to do anything that resembled work! The only complaint Roxey had with Seth's children was with Brandon... and it wasn't really a complaint. The boy just didn't seem to care for her. He wasn't rude. Only aloof.

In the four days she'd spent with the Dandridges, she'd been able to watch Seth with his children up close and in action. He approached everything as a learning opportunity—even something as mundane as weeding the garden. While they worked he would talk about each plant, what vitamins it contained, and how that vitamin contributed to their body's nutritional needs. The amount of knowledge the man carried around in his head was amazing!

Not only was he a good teacher, but he ran his home with an organization that rivaled that of the army. Housework was divided up and shared equally, and the amazing thing was it was done without argument! Roxey was impressed and readily admitted that Seth was qualified to instruct his children at home. He had shown her the textbooks he intended to use, and the lesson plans she'd examined were proof enough of the time he'd spent on preparation. Her one reservation was that—as far as she could see—the children had no opportunity to develop peer relationships—something Roxey considered vitally important.

Steam from the boiling pot billowed up, warming her face and reminding her of the job at hand. She swiped at the perspiration beading her forehead with the back of her wrist and returned her attention to her stirring. What she would give for an air conditioner about now! But at least she wasn't out in the sun with Brandon and Seth. She glanced out the door again.

Seth had pulled off his shirt and hung it on the lowest limb of the oak tree whose branches shaded part of the side yard. Roxey watched as he picked up a log and stood it on its end. When he raised the ax over his head, muscles bulged and rolled beneath the sweat-glistened skin stretching across his bare back. His feet were spread and one knee slightly cocked as his arms sliced down, the force of the swing pulling him to his toes. The ax hit the upended log, splitting it neatly in two. Roxey watched him repeat this process over and over and over until sweat poured in rivers down his chest and back. Mounds of split wood piled up faster than Brandon could move and stack them.

At last Seth drove the ax into the stump and reached for the jug of water he'd set in the shade of the oak tree. His Adam's apple bobbed up and down with each swallow as he drank long and deep. Water spilled out of the corners of his mouth and ran in tiny rivulets down his neck and chest. The sun's reflection caught the droplets of water clinging to his beard and turned them to shimmering diamonds.

How she'd hated that beard when she first met him, but now that she'd grown accustomed to it, Roxey couldn't imagine Seth any other way. When his tongue arced out to lick the drops of water from his mustache and lower lip, the spoon in her hand stilled. Her throat tightened, and she couldn't seem to work up enough saliva to swallow. More than six feet of solid man stood half-naked in front of her.

She felt like Eve standing in the Garden of Eden with that apple dangling temptingly in front of her, and that old snake whispering in her ear, *Just one bite. What'll it hurt?*

The heat was intense in the yard, but Seth much preferred it to the crowded kitchen and what would have been a forced proximity to Roxey. Especially after last night. It had taken every bit of his willpower to put her in her bed and not crawl in beside her. Her vulnerability had surprised him...and touched him. She'd seemed so small in his arms, so defenseless, filling him with an immense need to protect her. A feeling he hadn't experienced in a long time.

Seth wiped at the sweat on his forehead with the crook of his elbow before raising the ax high over his head to split another log. No time for daydreaming today. There was too much work that needed his attention.

A bloodcurdling scream came from the direction of the house, slicing across the still afternoon air. Already in midswing, Seth drove the ax through the log and deep into the stump in one powerful downward thrust before releasing it to run for the house. When he burst through the back door, he found Miss Bertha and Cissy crowded around Roxey.

Seth's booming voice cut across Miss Bertha's clucking sounds as she fussed over Roxey. "What happened?"

Cissy wheeled around, her eyes wide in alarm. "Miss Classen burned her hand."

Seth shouldered his way past Miss Bertha to kneel in front of Roxey. "Let me see."

A white towel was wrapped around her hand and she pulled it close to her waist, refusing to let him touch it. "No, it's nothing, really."

Miss Bertha clucked, "Nothing, my foot. She'll be lucky if it doesn't scar."

Seth caught the towel at its corner and gently unwound it. At the sight of the angry red blisters covering the back of her hand, a muscle in his jaw began to tick. He glanced up at her, his face tight with concern. "How'd it happen?"

Roxey felt her face color with a heat rivaling that rising from the still-boiling pot. "I was stirring the grape jelly and . . . well, uh, I guess I wasn't paying attention and it boiled over on my hand.''

He stood and started to walk away. ''Miss Bertha, get some ice on it. I'll get the salve out of the first-aid kit.'' As he passed by the stove, he stooped to pick up the spoon Roxey had dropped. Out of the corner of his eye something caught his attention, and he glanced out the door at his right. His shirt—still hanging on the limb of the tree— flapped in the light breeze as if it was waving at him.

Slowly he straightened and placed the spoon on the stove top. He glanced out the door again. A smile tugged at the corner of his mouth as he crossed the short hall to the bathroom. His reflection smiled back at him from the mirrored medicine cabinet door. He swelled out his chest like a strutting peacock. *So she wasn't paying attention, huh?* He rubbed his palm across the hairy surface of his chest. *And I wonder just what it was that captured Miss Classen's attention?* He chuckled at the thought, then his hand froze in midrub. *A gray hair?* He leaned closer to the mirror and looked again. Sure enough, several gray hairs lay nestled in the dark curling mass. He frowned as he yanked the door open, successfully blocking the reminder of his age.

You darn fool! Why would a sweet young thing like her look twice at an old country boy like you?

Loud voices carried up the stairs, under the door and straight to Roxey's ears. She flopped over on her side and pulled a pillow across her ear. Pain from the burns on her hand had kept her from sleeping well, and now her subconscious mind fought the intrusion to her sleep. The voices grew louder and louder, and she peeked out from underneath the pillow to the window beside her bed. It was still dark out. She slanted the alarm clock a one-eyed look and saw that it wasn't even 5:00 a.m. yet. *What on earth is going on?*

Not being a morning person even under normal circumstances, Roxey flounced off the bed and jerked on a robe. Stiff-legged she marched down the hall and stairs and through the swinging door to the kitchen. Just as she stepped inside, Seth slammed the back door behind a man.

"You are yelling loud enough to wake the dead! What in the world is wrong with you?" she demanded, now wide-awake and angry.

He plowed his fingers through already ruffled hair and glared back at her. "Nothing that concerns you."

"When I'm awakened at the crack of dawn, believe it or not, it concerns me." Roxey jerked out a chair from the kitchen table and sat down, her spine ramrod straight. She folded her arms at her waist. "So talk."

Seth spun a chair around and swung a leg across it, straddling the chair and resting his forearms along its back. He glared at her, his expression dark and forbidding. "That—" he jerked his head toward the back door "—was the man who was supposed to help me bale hay today."

"So?"

"So he's just coming in from a hard night drinking and isn't in any shape to do much of anything besides sleep it off."

"So?"

"So I can't *rake* hay and *bale* hay at the same damn time! Now do you get the picture?" He pushed off the chair, stomped to the stove and poured himself a cup of coffee.

"Isn't there someone else you can ask to help?"

Seth mocked her in a snide singsong voice. "No, there isn't someone else I can ask to help! If there were, I wouldn't be standing here carrying on this ridiculous conversation with you! I'd be asking them!"

Roxey jerked her robe up over her knee and crossed her legs. The man was impossible. Rude, hardheaded and downright cranky.

"Ted drunk again?"

Roxey's and Seth's heads both snapped around. Brandon stood in the doorway with one hand propping the swinging door open. His hair was ruffled and sleep still clogged his eyes.

"Yes, he's drunk again. Go on back to bed, son."

Brandon hitched up his pajama bottoms with his free hand, suddenly wide-awake and excited. "*I'll* drive for you Dad."

Seth smiled—the first smile Roxey had seen on his face in what seemed like days. "Thanks, son. But you're too young to be put up on a tractor."

"But, Dad. I've driven it before. You know I can do it. Come on, Dad. Please?"

"No, son. And that's final. Now go on back to bed."

Brandon shot Roxey a scowl. "I'll bet it's because you want *her* to drive for you."

The smile disappeared from Seth's face and a muscle tensed on his left jaw. "You get up those stairs right now before I'm tempted to turn you over my knee. Understand?"

Brandon ducked his head, but not before Roxey saw the angry look he shot her. "Yes, sir," he mumbled as he turned and let the door swing shut behind him.

Silence hung heavy in the kitchen for a full minute while Roxey thought over what Brandon had said. Obviously the boy didn't care much for her. He'd demonstrated that well enough in other instances over the past few days. But he was right about one thing—she could help out. "I'll drive the tractor."

Seth choked on the coffee he was sipping. "You?" He glanced at her bandaged hand. "Not with that hand."

Roxey worked the fingers back and forth. "It doesn't hurt anymore. I'm sure I could manage."

"But you don't know how to drive a tractor. You can't even drive a car!"

"If you're referring to the time my car slid off your road, I've already explained that I was avoiding a rabbit. I'll have you know I have an excellent driving record."

"Driving a car and a tractor are two entirely different things."

"They couldn't possibly be *that* different. After all, they both have a steering wheel."

An hour later Roxey sat on the hard iron seat of the ancient tractor and stared dumbfounded at the levers, buttons, gauges and dials in front of her, realizing just how different the two really were. Nothing looked even vaguely like something from the dashboard of her car. She pasted on a confident smile as she watched Seth walk toward her.

"Miss Bertha's here to watch the kids. You ready?" His voice was sharp with impatience.

"Yes, but maybe you'd better go over this one more time."

He pushed his cap farther back on his head and hitched his hands low on his hips. "Are you sure you want to do this? I can wait for Ted to sober up."

Roxey swallowed back her nervousness and attempted a weak smile. "No, really. I can do it." She looked back at the controls and her smile slowly wilted. *I may die trying, but I'll do it.*

And do it she did. Around and around and around the hay field she drove that rattly, bumpy, noisy, old tractor, dragging the massive rake behind her, piling up row after even row of freshly mown hay. It was like riding on a merry-go-round that wouldn't stop. Her head spun from the monotonous motion and she soon grew weary of the same scene repeated over and over and over again.

The only break in the pattern came when Seth passed her. He pulled the baler behind his tractor and Roxey found it fascinating to watch the baler work. Oversized forks scooped up the hay, and belts spun as the hay was compacted into tight square bales and spit out the back to fall in a neat line behind the baler. Even more fascinating to watch was the man driving the machine. His eyes were concealed from her by the brim of a green cap with John Deere emblazoned in a deep yellow that matched the yellow of the sunflowers growing wild at the perimeters of the field. Each time he crossed arm over arm to turn the enormous steering wheel, his broad shoulders strained beneath his faded University of Kentucky jersey. Roxey couldn't help envying him the blue mesh shirt. The airy fabric had to be cooler than the cotton she wore.

She sat up a little straighter to ease the pressure on her rear end. She felt like one big bruise from sitting on the iron seat while the tractor bounced over the uneven terrain.

Seth passed her on the inside circle and signaled for her to stop. She quickly ticked off his instructions; ease on the brake, then off the clutch, and pull back the biggest lever to stop the rake. A smile spread across her face as her movements created the desired effect.

She watched Seth jump over the huge rear tire on his tractor and groaned as she stretched and pressed a hand to the small of her back. How could he do it? She couldn't move. Her body felt as if it was paralyzed in this position.

Seth walked over to Roxey's tractor and leaned an elbow against the giant tire beside her. He pushed his cap back on his head and squinted up at the sun, deepening the crow's-feet at the corners of his eyes. "We've done about all there's time for today." He leaned over and patted her knee and gave her a wink. "You've done a good job. I don't know what I would've done without you."

Pride worked like bellows, swelling out her chest and pushing up a smile at her lips. She'd received trophies, awards and a dozen other forms of congratulations for a job well done, but none meant more to her than that simple wink and pat on the knee. The euphoric feeling surprised her and made her realize she'd unconsciously been trying to win his approval all week and had failed until now.

"I'll disconnect the rake and hook up the trailer to your tractor, then you can drive around the field while I load the bales onto the trailer. Okay?"

Roxey shuddered at the thought of circling the field even one more time, but forced a game smile. "Sure."

While he unhooked the rake, Seth explained the procedure. "Drive in low gear. Stop every second round or so and give me a chance to stack the bales I've loaded."

Roxey nodded her head. "Okay."

It took the remainder of the afternoon to load all the bales on the trailer. After stacking the last one, Seth climbed up on top of the hay and signaled Roxey to head for the barn. She waved her hand to acknowledge the signal and leaned forward to shift gears.

Finally they were going home! She was hot, tired and sweaty and wanted nothing more than a tall glass of iced tea, a hot bath and a soft bed—in that order.

In her excitement to leave the hay field, her foot slipped off the clutch while she was shifting gears. The tractor lunged forward then jerked to a stop. The unexpected motion whipped Roxey against the steering wheel, then back. From behind her she heard a loud curse and turned just in time to see Seth and the top two layers of hay topple off the side of the trailer.

Six

———

With shaking fingers Roxey yanked on the hand brake before jumping down and rushing over to Seth. He looked like a sleeping giant sprawled on the broken bales of hay.

Fear knotted her stomach and squeezed its icy fingers around her heart. What if she'd killed him? Her mind took off in ten different directions, but her feet refused to move. She quickly looked over his huge bulk. She couldn't possibly move him by herself. He was too big. She needed to get help.

Oh, God, what if he were dead? Her thoughts flew to Cissy and Brandon. How would she ever be able to tell them she'd killed their father? She wrung her hands. Oh, he was so still. Why didn't he move?

She knelt beside him and placed a tentative hand on his shoulder. "Seth?" When he didn't respond, she pressed three fingers against her quivering lips. Her voice cracked. "Oh, please, Seth. Answer me. Oh, God, I'll do anything. Just please don't let him die." Hot tears slid down her face, blinding her, and she wiped at them with the back of her wrist as she leaned over to place an ear to his chest.

"Anything?"

The word vibrated against her ear and cheek where they lay pressed against his chest. She raised her head and looked up into his face. His eyes were sparkling and a dimple winked at her from beneath his beard.

Why, the clod! He'd tricked her. Her fingers scratched up fistfuls of nylon fabric as she clenched her hands on his chest. Pushing off him, she struggled to her feet, seething. "You inconsiderate, mule-headed bear! I thought you were hurt... dead! And the whole time you were playing possum. That was a low-down rotten trick."

He laughed and his laughter angered her even more. "It's not funny! You scared me half out of my wits!" When he continued to laugh, she wheeled to leave him there, laughing and rolling in the hay like a fool. But just as she turned he caught her heel in his hand and pulled her down beside him. She landed facedown and came up sputtering, her mouth filled with bits of hay.

"Are you crazy?" she screeched. She grabbed a handful of the loose hay and threw it at him.

He ducked, then rolled over on top of her and pinned her to the ground, his hands clamped at her wrists above her head. His eyes sparkled with mischief.

"Probably."

His gaze drifted down the length of her that wasn't covered with his own body, then returned to her face. The wind and the sun had left Roxey's lips parched, and she ran her tongue across them to moisten them. She watched his gaze follow the path of her tongue and closed her eyes, preparing herself for the kiss she knew was sure to come.

When it didn't, she opened her eyes to his mischievous ones. Embarrassed, she tugged at her hands in frustration, but his grip was firm and she finally relaxed her struggles. "Well, are you having a good time?" she asked sarcastically.

"Um-hmm."

He eased her arms down until her elbows were even with her shoulders, then sat up a little straighter. She watched his gaze drift down to her stomach. Earlier in the day when the heat had been nearly unbearable, she had tied her shirttails up under her breasts, leaving a band of bare flesh exposed between her camp shirt and shorts. His penetrating gaze now burned her there. Her skin began to tingle. Why didn't he do something? Anything! "Why are you looking at me like that?"

"Yesterday you nearly got a third degree burn from looking at me without a shirt on. I was just wondering if it would be worth the pain to look at you without yours."

"Why you—" Roxey fought to free herself from his grip, twisting and turning beneath him. It only made her more aware of the part of his anatomy pressed against her thighs. She stopped her fighting and clenched her teeth, setting off a muscle to twitching on her jaw.

His mischievous smile drifted down, lower and lower, closer and closer until his lips brushed against hers. The coarse hair of his beard feathered against her cheek and chin. Roxey pressed her lips firmly together and lay perfectly still beneath him, her eyes fixed on the billowy clouds floating across the blue sky above his head.

Let him kiss all he wanted. She wasn't about to kiss him back. Not after that crack about her burning her hand while mooning over him. As if he were anything to look at!

Without moving her head, she lowered her gaze to sneak a glimpse of his chest. Dark hair tufted out of the opening of his faded jersey. She swallowed hard. Who was she trying to kid? He was definitely something to look at!

He framed her face with his hands while he nipped at her lips with his teeth. She felt her willpower dissolving, and her lips relaxed beneath his. Power and masculinity exuded from his every touch. From the feel of his lips on hers to the touch of his hands at her face. Yet there was a gentleness, a tenderness, too, that contrasted sharply with the aura of the man.

The kiss deepened and she felt his knees hug tighter against her hips. A kaleidoscope of emotions exploded within her. A part of her demanded to know why she was rolling in the hay with this mule-headed farmer, who for almost a week had alternately antagonized and ignored her. Yet another part of her wanted to let loose, to see where the kiss would lead.

He continued to move his lips against hers as he released his hold on her wrists to push his fingers through her hair. Though totally transfixed by the feel of him she couldn't help wondering what he wanted from her.

He skimmed his hand slowly down her neck to her breast, and all rational thought escaped her. She moved her fingers to the hem of his jersey and pulled up until her fingers met bare skin. Flattening her palms against the small of his back, she smoothed upward, bunching the mesh fabric higher on his back, then back down. Beneath her fingertips lay muscles developed and maintained from physical labor—not from working out in a health club like most of the men she knew.

Seth reached back over his shoulders and peeled his jersey over his head, then rolled to his side, pulling Roxey with him. As a homing pigeon seeks home, her fingers flew to his chest. Dark hair swirled and churned around each peaked nipple before rivering down his flat stomach and disappearing beneath his jeans. Her hands followed her gaze to the top button on the fly of his jeans. His stomach muscles tightened, allowing her to slide her fingers beneath the waistband.

She felt the swell in his jeans and a moistness in her own. So this is what it's like! she thought in wonder. She hoped her inexperience didn't show. For all her worldliness and boldness, Roxanne Classen was still a virgin.

When she brushed her fingers against his arousal, she lifted her gaze to his face. Dark, smoldering, effulgent eyes met hers. If only she knew proper sexual etiquette! Why hadn't they taught her *that* at finishing school? If they had, she wouldn't be lying here, wondering what to do next.

Now more than ever before Roxey regretted the years she'd spent as a tomboy, being best friends with all the guys, but never their girlfriend. Without being conscious of it at the time, she'd attempted to counteract her older sister's libidinous nature by going to the opposite extreme.

Her family had been shocked when she chose a baseball glove over dolls, and appalled when denim and fleece replaced the taffeta and lace usually found hanging in her closet. They consoled themselves by saying eventually she would grow out of this ''boyish'' stage.

Finishing school had softened her rough edges, and by the time she reached college, she'd escaped the tomboy stigma... but not the innocence it had left her with. Then in college her determination to be accepted in the family business had kept her nose in the books, leaving her little time for a social life. If she'd allowed herself the time to have a serious boyfriend, one she might have experimented and learned about sex with, she wouldn't have been in this awkward predicament now.

At long last she'd met the man who could arouse the woman in her, who made her yearn for his touch. And she wanted to please him in return. But she'd never felt so inadequate. Here she was, twenty-four years old and as inexperienced as... as LaVerne Higgenbotham!

She felt she would explode if Seth didn't do something soon. She wanted to tell him to make love to her. No, she wanted to *scream* at him to make love to her. But did a lady do that?

No words passed between them. The only sound in the meadow came from the birds singing, the wind whistling softly through the pines and Seth's labored breathing.

From above his shoulder, Roxey saw the late-afternoon sun hanging at treetop level, looking as if it had snagged there on its downward slide. A soft breeze wafted across the meadow carrying scents of pine and freshly mown hay, chasing away the summer heat and leaving an early-evening coolness hanging over all.

Seth didn't notice the coolness. God help him, but he burned with his need for her! And she needed him. He knew she did. Every part of her body cried out for his touch. Lips as sweet and ripe as any fruit. Round, full breasts, thrusting against the confines of her thin cotton blouse. Hips that rubbed and teased against his thigh. Fevered skin that burned beneath his touch.

He moved his hands to cup her face and pulled her to him. Their lips met and locked together as he rolled her to her back and threw a knee across her thighs.

Sprigs of hay cut into her back, and Seth's leg felt like lead on Roxey's, but it didn't matter. New sensations pulled at her, making her forget the discomfort, making her want this moment to go on forever. She wrapped her arms around his neck and pressed her body against his. But she couldn't get close enough. Fully knowing it was impossible, she couldn't suppress the desire to be inside of him, one with him.

Her wigglings thrust her hip full against Seth's groin, drawing a low groan from deep within him. He felt her breasts flatten against his chest, and he tightened his own arms around her. She was so small, so fragile compared to him. He feathered kisses over her face and neck, tasting the soft, sweet nectar of her skin. He trailed his lips over her chin and down her neck to the first button on her blouse.

He slipped his hand from beneath her to work each button from its hole, then moved it lower to free the knot below her breasts. Lips replaced fingers as the blouse fell open. A thin lace bra barred him from being skin to skin, and he shifted his body to unfasten it to suckle at the hard pink tips straining toward him.

When his mouth closed over her breast, electrical currents shot through Roxey, from her breast to her lower abdomen, surging through her with a liquid fire. She heard a moan and felt heat burn her cheeks when she realized it was her own. She wanted something from him and would have asked for it . . . if only she'd known what to ask for.

While he moved to suckle at her other breast, he eased his fingers down to the snap on her shorts. Cool air hit her when the zipper slid down, exposing bare skin, then heat when his fingers spread across her abdomen.

He rubbed his thumb in small circles lower and lower down her abdomen until he bumped against the elastic of her bikini panties. Roxey sucked in her lower lip and bit down on it as shivers chased down her spine and all the way to her toes.

Her body lay soft and inviting beneath him as he worked his hand between her silk panties and the snug-fitting shorts. But when he slipped his fingers between her thighs, Roxey's body tensed and she dug her fingernails into his back.

When Roxey tensed, so did Seth. Something was wrong. He could feel it in his gut. Surely she wasn't . . . Slowly he withdrew his hand and sat up beside her, his chest rising and falling in quick grabbing breaths.

Roxey felt a little sick to her stomach as she watched him sit up and turn his back to her. "Did I do something wrong?"

"Wrong?" he echoed, his voice almost too quiet. "No. You didn't do anything wrong." He picked up a piece of hay and twirled it between his fingers for a moment before cocking his head to look at her, his look piercing her with its intensity. "If I ask you a question, will you give me an honest answer?"

She forced herself to meet his gaze as she sat up and pulled her blouse together. "Yes."

"Are you a virgin?"

Roxey's fingers froze on her buttons. "Why?"

"I need to know."

Her fingers felt like blocks of wood as she forced them to work the buttons on her blouse. "What difference does it make?"

Seth threw down the hay and twisted around to face her, his eyes dark and angry. "A hell of a lot!"

With her back straight and her head held proud, she met his angry gaze. "Yes, I'm a virgin."

He hit the flat of his hand to his forehead. "Damn! Why didn't you tell me?"

"I didn't know it was a prerequisite to making love with you." She adjusted her shorts as she bit back the tears of humiliation and hurt that suddenly burned behind her eyes.

He saw the moisture building in her eyes and quickly looked away. Why did she always have to cry? It made him feel about as useless as a steer in a pasture full of spring heifers. He rested his wrists on propped-up knees and ducked his head between them. Slowly he counted from one to ten, then back to one and let out a long frustrated breath.

There was no reason to be mad at her. It wasn't *her* fault she was a virgin. He chuckled softly at the ridiculous thought. Well, whose fault was it if it wasn't hers? One thing for sure, it wasn't his. If he had his choice in the matter, she wouldn't be one for long.

He stole a glance in her direction and saw she had straightened her clothes and was brushing at the hay sticking to her hair. Even sitting in a pile of hay with her hair all messed up and straw sticking out all over, she still managed to look beautiful—and as regal as any queen. She deserved more than a haystack her first time. But he could tell by the defensive lift of her chin, she wouldn't believe him if he tried to explain. She was hurt and maybe a little angry.

Seth stood and brushed at the hay clinging to his chest. The best thing to do would be to ignore the situation, to pretend nothing happened. In two steps he covered the distance between them and stood in front of her, one hand stretched out to help her up. She glanced at the hand a moment, then almost reluctantly placed hers in his. With a quick tug he pulled her to stand beside him, then just as quickly dropped it and began to restack the unbroken bales of hay.

When Roxey gained the courage to steal a glance his way, she saw he still wore the ridiculous half grin she had seen appear on his face just moments ago. How could he possibly find anything humorous in this humiliating mess? Her checks burned with embarrassment at her lack of experience and his subsequent rejection. Right then and there, Roxanne Classen made a vow. She would *never* be caught in a situation like this again! Seth Dandridge—whether he wanted to or not—would teach her all he knew about making love and, in the bargain, would receive her virginity. How she would persuade him to do so, she wasn't sure. But she would. Of that she was certain!

Roxey had nearly worn a path in the floor of her room from her pacing. She sat down on the rocker beside her bed, then popped right up again. How should she go about handling this? Should she just go down to his room and crawl into his bed? Or should she wake him up and ask his permission first?

With a groan she flopped down on the rocker, squeezing her hands between her knees. One thing was for sure. It would have to be tonight, because tomorrow morning she would be going back to Louisville... and she had no intention of going back a virgin.

With a forced calm, she rose and straightened her nightgown. It was now or never. Determination carried her down the stairs, through the hall and into his bedroom. Fear stopped her short at the side of his bed.

Moonlight shining through the undraped window spilled across the bed, illuminating his sleeping form. Both of his hands were pushed deep beneath his pillow, bunching up the muscles on his back. Her hand itched to touch the wide expanse, to smooth a palm across the breadth of it, to feel the strength of the man. His back was bare to his waist where a sheet glared stark white against his tanned skin. Was he naked beneath the sheet? Her hands flew to her cheeks. Oh, Lord! Could she really go through with this? Before she lost her courage, she stretched out shaky fingers to touch his shoulder.

"Seth?"

Immediately he was awake and twisting to sit up in bed, catching the sheet low at his waist. He focused on Roxey's pale face. "Is Cissy sick?" He blinked several times, then rubbed his eyes to clear the sleep from them.

Roxey ducked her head. "No. No, Cissy isn't sick."

"Brandon?"

"No. Not Brandon."

His voice turned sharp with impatience. "Well, what's wrong then?"

Roxey dug her toes into the rug beside his bed and clasped her hands in a tight fist behind her. "I wanted to talk to you."

He glanced at the clock beside the bed and fell back against the pillow, covering his eyes with his forearm. "Couldn't it wait till morning?"

"No, it couldn't." Irritation made her voice sharp. This was tough enough without his acting so contrary. "When we were in the hay meadow the other day, you asked me if I was a virgin." She laced her fingers together, then studied the nail of her left thumb. "Well, I don't want to be one anymore."

If he heard what he thought he heard, he must be sleeping and this was some kind of dream—or nightmare. Seth lifted his arm a fraction from his eyes and peeked out. Sure enough, there she stood beside his bed, wearing some flimsy nightgown and looking for all the world as if she would bolt and run if he so much as said "boo."

With the sheet gripped tightly in his hands, he slowly pushed himself to a sitting position and dropped his wrists over his knees. The word *honor* was a term associated with knights and gentlemen, never with the name Seth Dandridge. And he hadn't been with a woman in the biblical sense for longer than he cared to remember. He glanced up, and his gaze rested on the slow rise and fall of her breasts. He felt a quiver in his groin as he remembered how it had felt to touch her there and squeezed his eyes shut against the tempting sight. Damn! He wanted this woman bad! Then why in the hell was he sitting here trying to think up reasons to get her to go back to her room, instead of taking what she so freely offered?

Because he cared. That was why. The realization surprised him. With a barely discernible lift of his index finger he gestured to the foot of the bed. "Sit down."

Her back rigid, Roxey sat on the very edge of the mattress but found it impossible to look at him. Instead, she focused her attention on the window to his right.

"Why do you want to lose your virginity?"

The question drew her gaze to his then quickly away again. She squeezed her hands together in her lap. "I'm twenty-four years old. Don't you think it's about time?"

He reached over and plucked her hand from her lap and pressed it between his palms. Surprised at the tender gesture, she glanced up at his face. In the moonlight his eyes seemed to lose their brooding darkness and take on a softer, warmer cast as they looked deeply into hers.

"There's no such thing as a certain time, Roxey. It's the circumstances that count." He studied his thumb as he rubbed it back and forth against the side of hers in a slow caress. "You need to be with the man you love. And it's not something you plan. When the time's right, it just happens."

Her mouth sagged open, and she quickly clamped it shut. She loved him. The realization didn't surprise her nearly as much as the amount of time it had taken for her to recognize it. Quickly, she turned her head away, for fear he could read her thoughts on her face.

Roxanne Classen in love. It was almost funny. The girl who had avoided serious relationships for years was finally in love ... and with a man who wouldn't take her virginity even when it was offered to him on a silver platter. And with no strings attached!

"Don't cry, Cissy." Roxey knelt in front of the small child and thumbed away a tear from her cheek.

"But I'll miss you, Miss Classen."

"I'll miss you, too, Cissy. But we'll see each other next week when you come to my house."

"Promise?"

"Promise." Roxey hugged the little girl to her, then sat back on her heels and tilted Cissy's face up with the tip of her finger. "And I'll have all kinds of fun things for us to do. Okay?"

"Okay." Cissy sniffed, then swiped at her wet cheeks with the back of her wrist.

Roxey stood and stepped to Brandon, stretching out her hand to him. "Thank you, Brandon, for teaching me how to feed the chickens and horses."

After receiving a prod in the back from his father, Brandon reluctantly pulled his hand from his pocket, shook Roxey's, then quickly stuffed his hand back into his pocket with a mumbled, "You're welcome."

Another step and she stood in front of Seth. Last night's confrontation had left an awkwardness between them, one both of them were having a hard time dealing with. She forced herself to smile. "I've had a wonderful week. Thanks for inviting me."

"You're welcome to visit anytime."

She had the wildest urge to throw herself into his arms and tell him she loved him and beg him to let her stay. Instead she extended her hand. "See you next week?"

He clasped her hand in his. "Yeah. Saturday." With a quick squeeze he released her hand and stepped behind Cissy, placing his hands on his daughter's small shoulders.

Roxey climbed into the car and shut the door. With shaking fingers she tried to fit the key into the ignition. She glanced out the side window where three Dandridges blurred before her. God, how she hated to leave them! In one short week she had experienced so much, and had been surrounded by more love than ever in her life . . . and she was reluctant to leave it all behind.

Seth saw the pain in her eyes, and it filled him with regret, for the pain he saw matched the one knotting his gut as he watched her drive away.

Seven

Seth shuffled along the bricked sidewalk leading to Roxey's town house with butterflies the size of cave bats flapping in his stomach. With each step he assured himself it was okay to be there. After all, she had invited them.

Stalling for time, he stopped and looked up at the sky, shading his eyes against the sun's blinding rays. Not a cloud in the sky held a promise of rain to cool things off. He tilted his head back farther to watch a hot-air balloon float by overhead and felt a thin river of perspiration course down the middle of his back. Damn it was hot! But was it the heat or Roxey that had him feeling so uncomfortable? Not willing to dwell on that thought, Seth pushed it out of his mind and walked on toward her house.

The front stoop of the town house was about the size of a postage stamp, but Seth accepted what little shade it offered. He pushed the doorbell and frowned as he listened to the musical chimes echo through the house. It was the kind of sound a person expected would be followed by some butler swinging the door wide and saying, "You rang, sir?" But no butler responded to this ring.

Impatient, he really leaned on the button this time, holding it down for several seconds before releasing it, then giving it a few quick jabs for good measure. He stepped back and waited.

Heat from the glaring sun burned into his shirt, turning the thin river of perspiration running down his back into a flood. *Come on, Roxey. Don't leave me out here to melt.* He held his elbows akimbo to give what little breeze there was a chance to dry the damp circles beneath his armpits, and thanked the good Lord he didn't live in this cement-encrusted city.

He hadn't been in Louisville thirty minutes, and already he missed his farm. The drive through town on the traffic-clogged freeway was enough to make him thankful he didn't have to fight this rat race anymore. Everybody in a hurry to get nowhere. How he hated it!

A fumbling sound on the other side of the door drew his attention just before the door swung open. Roxey stood in the doorway with one hand clutching the front of a gauzy cover-up, while she struggled to slip her arm into the sleeve. Before she managed to pull it on, Seth caught a glimpse of bare skin and bikini.

Wide blue eyes met his dark ones. "Seth. You're early." She stood on tiptoe to peer around him. "Where are the children?"

"At their mother's." He watched her brows wrinkle into a puzzled frown and quickly added, "Hope you don't mind the change in plans, but Lorissa wanted them to spend the afternoon and have dinner with her. Since they hadn't seen her in a while, I said it was okay."

Though she hid it well, his hurried explanation dashed the hope out of Roxey. When she saw him standing there alone, for a second she had imagined he'd arranged it that way, that he'd missed her as much as she'd missed him. But it appeared he had come only to tell her of the change in plans. "Oh, I see."

A heat built on his face rivaling the one searing his back. Maybe this hadn't been such a good idea, after all. All the way to her house, he had rationalized that it only made sense for him to go on alone. After all, she was expecting them. But now that he was here, he could see it had been a mistake.

"Well, I guess we'll see you later tonight." He turned and had taken one step down before Roxey's voice stopped him.

"What will you do while the children are at their mother's?"

He shoved his hands into the pockets of his jeans as he glanced back at her. "Oh, I don't know. Maybe see a movie or something."

Roxey stepped out onto the porch, garnering her courage. "You could wait here."

"I wouldn't want to put you out or anything."

"Oh, no, you wouldn't be. I was just sunbathing by the pool. Do you have your luggage?"

"Yeah, it's in the truck."

"If you brought your bathing suit, you could go for a swim if you want."

Seth wiped at the sweat beading his forehead and breathed a deep sigh of relief as he squinted up at the sun. "Sounds like heaven to me."

Had he actually thought this would be heaven? After half an hour poolside, Seth felt more as if he had plunked himself down in the fiery bowels of hell. The heat searing him now was different from the one he'd experienced while waiting on Roxey's front stoop—one not so easily escaped.

Stretched out on a lounge chair, he had a perfect rear view of Roxey bobbing slowly up and down on a raft in the middle of the pool. Water lapped at the sides of her legs and waist in a slow undulating tide and pooled in the recess between her thighs. With each pulse of the water, Seth felt himself drawn toward her, then sucked back with each ebb.

His gaze drifted from her toes, hanging off one end of the bright yellow raft, to her fingers, drifting through the water at the other end, and then back to the water beading in the gentle curve of her back. Her skin glistened golden brown with oil, and even from this distance he could smell the oil's coconut fragrance.

"How come you don't freckle?"

Using one hand as a paddle and the other as a rudder, Roxey smoothly turned the raft until she faced him. "Should I?"

"Most redheads do."

She bent one leg at the knee, her toe pointing up to the sky, and smiled a lazy smile. "I guess I'm just lucky."

The movement drew Seth's gaze to the soft curve of her ankle, down the gentle slope of her calf, to the water between her thighs. Sweat popped out on his forehead. "Yeah, I guess you are."

Oblivious to the effect her movements were having on him, Roxey scooped up a palmful of water and splashed it against her neck, allowing it to run down her chest to disappear in the valley between her breasts. "It's *so* hot today!"

He swallowed against the lump threatening to choke him. "Yeah. It is."

"The weatherman said it's the hottest July in twenty years."

It was definitely the hottest one Seth had spent in a while—and he wasn't thinking in terms of the sun! A jump in the pool was what he needed to cool off. He rolled to his feet and walked to the diving board. He bounced once, twice, three times against the sandpaper-rough surface before he propelled his body up and away from the board. Looping his arms around his knees and pulling them up tight against his chest, he performed a precision cannonball, landing within inches of Roxey, and successfully drenching her.

When he surfaced at the head of her raft, she was still spitting water.

"You rat! I didn't want to get wet!"

Seth's mouth sagged open. "Not get wet? What are you doing in the pool if you didn't want to get wet?"

In an attempt to save her makeup, Roxey dabbed at the water around her eyes before glaring at him. "Sunbathing." She held out her finger and saw that it was smudged with black. And to think she'd spent an hour before the mirror applying all this just for him. "And just look. My mascara's running."

"Now isn't that a shame." Seth smiled sweetly before slipping beneath the water's clear blue surface. Roxey leaned over to peer beneath the water, her eyes widening in alarm as she watched him swim under her raft. He wouldn't. But when it became obvious he certainly would, she screeched, "Don't you dare!"

Ignoring her, Seth pushed upward with all his strength and sent the raft shooting into the air, Roxey with it, her arms and legs beating the air like a windmill on a windy day. On the downward fall, her bottom smacked the water first, but before her head plunged beneath the surface, she sucked in a deep gulp of precious air.

Water burned in her nose as she plummeted to the bottom of the pool, where strong arms circled her. As she twisted around to meet Seth's laughing eyes, the smoothness of her thighs brushed against the hairy coarseness of his. The teasing laughter slowly faded from his eyes, and he pulled her up against him, trapping her arms between them.

Water swirled around them, pulsing at their most private places, caressing them while wrapping them in a silky cocoon of silence. As his lips touched hers, he gently pushed off the bottom of the pool with his toes. Bubbles of air appeared between them, tickling their faces before breaking away to race them to the surface.

Their heads broke through the water's surface at the same instant, their lips still locked together while rivulets of water ran down their faces, blinding them. Two sets of feet frantically kicked to keep them afloat while two sets of arms refused to relinquish their hold on the other.

Need for air finally forced them apart, but only far enough and long enough to allow needed oxygen to pass through. He pressed his mouth to hers again, nipping and biting and kissing in wild abandon.

Gradually the urgency disappeared, and his lips moved across hers in breathtaking slowness. He kept one arm around her, while he swam with the other using deep, strong strokes to guide them to the shallower end of the pool.

At a point where he could touch bottom, he stopped swimming and stood with his feet braced against the floor of the pool and Roxey against his body. He caught the length of her hair in his hands and pulled firmly, masterfully, until her face turned up to his. "I've missed you, Roxey."

"I've missed you, too." She leaned back, framing his face with her hands, her thumbs pressed into the dimples on his cheeks. This was the moment she'd been dreaming of since the day she left his farm. Her gaze met his, open, pleading...trusting.

"Make love to me, Seth."

His fingers tensed in her hair as his gaze searched her face. "Do you realize what you're asking?"

At first she only nodded, then her lips parted on a whispered, "Yes."

A low growl erupted from deep within him as Seth scooped her up and waded with long strides from the pool. Water dripped from his hair and beard onto the broad, muscled planes of his chest and back. Dressed in a swimsuit, his bare feet slapping against the pebbled finish of the deck, he reminded Roxey of a caveman, dragging his woman off to his cave. The only item missing from this comical image was the club. Roxey laced her fingers around his neck and settled against his chest with a deep sigh. No, Seth Dandridge didn't need a club where Roxanne Classen was concerned. She would follow him anywhere.

When they reached her bedroom, Seth grinned down at her. "I'm dripping water all over the floor."

"I don't care."

She felt his chuckle against her cheek.

"How do you feel about getting your bed wet?"

"I don't care about that, either."

His chuckle grew to a laugh. "And coconut oil?"

Roxey glanced from the satin comforter covering her bed to her oil-slick skin and frowned.

"That's what I thought." He continued across the deep-piled carpeting of her bedroom, passing the queen-size bed, and on toward the bathroom. Roxey glanced back over his shoulder at the bed. What in the world was he doing? The bed was the other direction!

He released her to stand in the middle of the bathroom floor while he pulled open the shower door and turned on the taps full blast. Steam billowed over the top of the door, swirling around the room and quickly fogging the mirror. Wide-eyed and breathless, Roxey remained where Seth had placed her and waited while he pulled towels from the linen closet and tossed them to the tiled floor beside the shower door. When he turned around, he glanced at Roxey, his fingers growing still on the drawstring at his waist.

"Aren't you going to take your swimsuit off?"

A heat began to pulse in her face. She'd never undressed in front of a man, and in broad daylight yet! "Tell you what," she said nervously, "you shower first while I go make us a glass of iced tea." She spun around, but Seth caught her hand before she had a chance to escape.

He pulled her to his lap as he sat down on the edge of the marble bathtub. His arms circled her while he nuzzled against her neck with first his nose, then his lips. "I'm sorry, Roxey. I forget you're new at this."

She sat rigid in his lap, every muscle in her body tensed, too embarrassed to acknowledge his apology. He massaged her shoulders, working at the tense muscles with the balls of his thumbs. "It's okay, Roxey. We'll go slow." He pressed his lips against the soft skin between her shoulder blades, sending a shiver coursing down her spine as he stroked her arms, taking the straps of her bikini with him.

Warm moist air from the steaming shower pressed around her, beading her skin with a light film of perspiration. He kissed the side of her neck and she dipped her head to her opposite shoulder, giving him better access to the sensitive skin. Tense muscles began to relax as the heat of his kiss increased. She turned in his lap, resting her hands on his shoulders, her forehead against his. His breath blew warm against her chin while he fumbled with the bikini's hook at her back and she felt the fabric fall away.

He slipped her off his lap to stand in front of him, and with her hands balanced on his shoulders, he was almost at eye level with her navel. Slowly he lifted his gaze to her face. "You're beautiful, Roxey."

When she looked away in embarrassment, he forced her face back to his. "Never be ashamed of your body." Heat began to build in her eyes as his gaze continued to hold hers, and he slipped his hands to her hips. He eased the bikini bottoms over the fullest part of her hips and tugged gently, then let the fabric fall to pool at her ankles.

He stood then and held her hand as she stepped out of them. His voice came low and husky. "Would you like to undress me?"

Her eyes grew large, and she bit at her lower lip a moment before raising her hands to fumble with the drawstring at his waist. Shyness squeezed her eyes shut, but a wantonness she didn't know she possessed kept her fingers at his waist, tugging and working until she felt the damp suit fall away. The shower door snapped open, and the blast of hot steam forced her eyes open again. Seth stood naked before her with one foot in the shower and a hand outstretched to her.

Taking a deep breath, she placed a shaky hand in his and stepped inside. A thick cloud of steam quickly enveloped them as the door snapped shut behind them. Seth enfolded her in his arms, pulling her back snug against his arousal. She turned in his arms and stood on tiptoe to mold her body to his. Squared pads of muscled chest pressed against her cheek, offering warmth and security within his embrace. All embarrassment and hesitation fled as she felt his arms tighten around her. This was where she wanted to be. This was where she was meant to be...in Seth Dandridge's arms.

With Roxey's naked body molded against his, hot needles of desire, as piercing as the needles of spray pelting his skin, pricked Seth, building within him a want, a desire, a need greater than any he'd ever known. More surprising to him was the accompanying desire to please Roxey, and it was this need that enabled him to hold back the demands of his own passion to concentrate on hers.

While steam whirled and churned around them he smoothed his hands over her skin, washing away the traces of coconut oil and teaching Roxey the pleasures a mere touch could bring. Gradually, her need to share that feeling overshadowed her timidity, and with her gaze locked with his, she took the bar of scented soap and lathered her hands. Beginning at the broad plane of his shoulders, she moved over him in mind-drugging strokes, working her way across his chest, circling his nipples with the soapy tip of one finger, then smoothing downward to his waist.

His eyes drifted closed as a shudder passed through his body. He caught her hands in his and pulled them to clasp at the back of his waist, then circled her with his arms, laying his cheek against her damp hair, his lips at her temple. Soap bubbles exploded between them as he pulled her body flush against his. His breath blew warm and ragged against her fevered skin as he whispered, "Feel what you do to me, woman?"

Woman. Yes, she was a woman, with a woman's needs and a woman's desires. Roxey answered his question with a tremulous nod and together they stepped from the shower and hurriedly dried off before Seth scooped her up in his arms and carried her to the bedroom.

Late afternoon sun streamed through the undraped panes of the French doors, turning the peach-colored walls of Roxey's bedroom a deeper melon and setting the peach satin comforter Seth had carelessly pushed to the foot of the bed ablaze with color. Those same fiery colors danced through

Roxey's hair, haloing her face on the pure white sheets where Seth had placed her.

"Are you protected, Roxey?"

A worried frown knitted her brow. "No, I hadn't thought—"

"Don't worry. I'll take care of it." Seth left the room, and Roxey listened to his muffled movements in the guest room beside hers. He returned moments later.

Stretching out on his side next to her, Seth rested one hand at her waist while threading the fingers of his other hand through her hair. Showering with Roxey had been a sweet torture, one he hadn't been sure he would survive, but one he knew was necessary. Besides the fact that she was as slick as a greased pig with all that suntan lotion, he knew a shower would give her added time to become more familiar with her own sexuality...and maybe the time to reconsider. His own doubts made him search her face with his gaze as he asked one last time, "Are you sure, Roxey?"

She'd never been more sure of anything in her life. She met his questioning look with confidence. "Yes, I'm sure."

His breath was labored as he struggled to control his own need, his voice low and serious. "It's not too late. We could end this right here before any damage is done and I wouldn't blame you."

The man was surely a saint. Here he was trying to save her virginity, while she was doing all she could to lose it. She didn't bother to respond to his unselfish though unnecessary offer, but instead laced her fingers behind his neck and, with a slow seductive smile, pulled him to her.

Their lips met, cool and moist after the heat from the shower's steam—his reluctant still, hers hungry and inquisitive. Determined to convince him she knew what she wanted, Roxey caught his lower lip lightly between her teeth and nipped at it before drawing it between her lips. Innate yearnings guided her, and she allowed herself the freedom to satisfy them all.

She wanted to know the feel of his skin, to allow her fingers to travel each bulge and valley where well-honed muscles worked beneath it. She wanted to bury herself in his arms, soaking up all the love and affection he had to offer. She wanted him to fill this hollow ache deep within her and soothe away the throbbing pulse between her legs.

Seth groaned as she pressed her leg against his thigh. For weeks, almost since the day they'd met, Seth had known this moment was inevitable but had successfully resisted temptation...until now. Passionate fires, banked too long, flared, demanding satisfaction. His need for her became a physical pain, yet he continued to stall. She was so delicate. The thought of causing her pain made him pull slightly away. "Roxey, this may hurt."

Her fingers grew still at his back then slowly tightened as she nodded. "I know."

He touched his fingers to her flushed cheeks, then let them drift down, searing a line from her cheek to her hip. Roxey's breath caught in her throat. It was almost more than she could stand. His very touch sent tendrils of fire shooting through her body, fire she knew could only be extinguished by this man beside her. She watched the light in his eyes simmer, then blaze as he shifted her body to match the curve of his.

"It's going to be good between us, Roxey. I can promise you that."

Then he brought his mouth to hers, urging her lips apart while he slipped his hand over her breast.

He felt her tremble beneath his touch, but knowing the pleasure he could give her, Seth took her aroused nipple between his fingertips and lightly squeezed and rolled it until she writhed beneath him.

Roxey had never known a man could bring a woman to such heights. She arched beneath his hand, silently begging for more of his touch. He slid his free hand up and down her body, stroking and caressing while a liquid fire poured through her. When he at last touched the spot that pulsed with her need for him, her lips parted beneath his, emitting a groan, and he slipped his tongue into her mouth while he sought her waiting moistness with his fingertips.

Wanting only to know this man, to give him the pleasure he so readily gave to her, Roxey smoothed her hands down the wide expanse of his back. Her fingertips dipped at the curve of his waist, then rose to cup the rounded swell of his hips.

Unable to hold back any longer, Seth moved against her, easing himself into her, gradually increasing the pressure until he felt her fingernails dig into his flesh and saw the muscles of her face tense.

"It's okay, Roxey. Relax." His voice soothed, yet the pressure increased until she was sure she wouldn't be able to encompass him. She pressed her hands into tight fists at his shoulders and turned her head to the side, trying to suppress the soft whimpers escaping her lips. Then she felt him slide deep within her. His mouth came down, closing over hers, smothering her low moan. He lay still and covered her face with a rapid fire of kisses, continuing to murmur soothing words to her as he pressed burning lips to her forehead, her eyelids, her cheeks, then back to her lips. "It's okay, Roxey. It's okay now. It won't hurt anymore, I promise. Trust me, Roxey."

Then he began to move his hips against her, slowly at first, urging her to follow him in a sensual dance. The pain gradually faded to a distant blur as her hips moved beneath him. The pace increased, driving Roxey higher and higher, faster and faster, until it seemed the whole room moved in whirling rhythm with them. She clung to Seth, her chest heaving as she gasped for each breath.

Then suddenly everything slammed to a stop with Seth's last deep thrust. The room exploded with color, swirling and changing like the pieces of glass in a kaleidoscope, and Roxey felt herself spiraling down in a whirlwind of sensation. Still intimately joined with him, she closed her eyes and allowed her body and mind to savor the sweet pleasure of being in Seth's arms.

After a moment, Seth lifted his head and smiled at her. He shifted his weight from her, then tucked her protectively at his side. Roxey closed her eyes again and snuggled near to him. Never had she felt this complete, this content. She tightened her hold on him, glorying in the strength of his embrace.

Dusk's first shadows played around the corners of the room as Roxey slowly awoke. A heavy weight seemed to be holding her down and she lifted her head to see what imprisoned her. A slow smile started on her face as she saw Seth's arm draped across her waist. As if he sensed her discomfort, he pulled his arm away and slipped it underneath his pillow. Her smile built until she was sure she would swallow her face if she smiled much bigger. She stretched her toes out toward the foot of the bed and her fingers to the carved headboard. Some things in life were definitely worth waiting for!

She rolled to her side to face him, curling her fists under her cheek, still not quite believing he was really here. But there he was, stretched out on his stomach with his hands shoved deep under his pillow, his shoulders hunched forward, bunching up the muscles on his back. Tanned skin glowed a golden brown in the waning light, contrasting sharply with the stark white sheet draped seductively at his waist.

She lifted her gaze from his waist to the side of his face exposed to her. Careful not to wake him, she reached out a tentative hand and partially covered his beard with her fingers, squinting her eyes and trying to imagine what he would look like with it properly trimmed. She moved her hand to his hair and tucked the too long strands behind his ear, then gently smoothed it back across the nape of his neck. Satisfied with her experiment, she drew her hand back and dropped her chin onto her open palm.

With a little polish, Seth Dandridge could be a handsome man, she was sure. Why he chose to look and act like some uneducated hillbilly was beyond her comprehension!

Even in the rough he was easy to look at, and he definitely wasn't missing any important parts. She smiled again at the thought.

He stirred and opened one eye to squint at her. "What time is it?"

Roxey glanced at the bedside clock beyond Seth. "Almost seven."

He groaned as he stretched out his arms, locking his elbows and pushing against the headboard. "I've got to get up."

"Why?"

"The kids. I told Lorissa I'd pick 'em up about seven-thirty."

By avoiding his gaze, Roxey tried to hide her disappointment. She hated to have their intimacy interrupted—even by the arrival of the children. It was a selfish desire at best, but one she couldn't help. This was the first opportunity they'd really had to be alone, and Roxey wasn't ready to relinquish him again and have to compete with the children for his attention and his time.

She forced a smile as she looked back at him. "Do you want me to go with you?"

Seth rolled to his side to face her, his movement dragging the sheet away from Roxey. A lazy smile tugged at the corner of his mouth as he let his gaze travel from her eyes to her knees, then back to her eyes. "Dressed like that?"

With a boldness that surprised her, Roxey glanced from her nudeness to his, pausing a moment at the bulge pushing at the sheet just below his waist before lifting her gaze to his. "I might grab a pair of shoes first."

A deep chuckle shook the bed as Seth reached for her. With his arms wrapped around her, he squeezed her to him, sighing deeply. "Oh, Rox. You're special. Do you know that?"

"Um-hm." Scooting closer, she snuggled up against him.

Breathing in the warm fragrance of her hair, Seth drew small nervous circles on her bare back with his fingertips. "You aren't sorry, are you, Roxey?"

He felt her smile against his chest. "No. I'm not sorry." She leaned her head back until she could see his face. "Are you?"

His eyes searched hers before he slipped his hand to the back of her neck and pulled her head to cradle beneath his chin. "I hope not. Oh, God, I hope not."

Eight

Here are the baseball tickets. And these passes will get you into the locker room to meet the players. Cissy and I'll meet you back here after the game. Oh, and just in case—'' Roxey dug around in her purse and pulled out a key ''—here's a key to the house.''

Seth slipped the tickets into his shirt pocket before taking the key from Roxey. A worried frown furrowed his brow. "Why do we need a key? Won't you and Cissy be here when we get back?"

"Probably, but just to be sure, take it with you."

"Where are y'all going?"

Roxey laughed at Seth's battery of questions. "I'm not kidnapping her. We're going shopping."

"Oh."

Noticing his worried frown, Roxey quickly asked, "That's okay, isn't it?"

"Yeah, sure. I just thought y'all would probably stay here." He knelt in front of Cissy, cupping her shoulders with his hands. "You be a good girl, Cissy, and stay right with Miss Classen. I don't want you getting lost. Okay?"

"Okay, Daddy." Cissy giggled as she caught his beard in her hands and pushed her face close against his. "And you stay close to Brandon. I wouldn't want *you* getting lost, either."

"Smarty-pants." With a quick kiss, he tweaked her nose before standing to offer one more admonition. "And don't talk to any strangers."

Cissy rolled her eyes. "Oh, Daddy."

"Well, you can't be too careful."

Roxey caught Seth by the arm and guided him toward the front door where Brandon waited. "I promise to bring your daughter home in one piece. Now if you don't scoot, you two are going to miss the first pitch."

At the door Seth turned a doubtful face in Cissy's direction. "Are you sure you two don't want to see the Louisville Redbirds play?"

In unison Cissy's and Roxey's voices sang out, "Yes, we're sure."

With one last long look, Seth backed out the door, pulling it closed on his worried expression.

Roxey turned to Cissy with an exasperated sigh. "Is he always like this when you do something without him?"

"Only when we're in Louisville."

Shopping was probably the least favorite of Roxey's pastimes. It rated somewhere below cleaning bathrooms and having cavities filled. Unfortunately, Cissy proved to be the exact opposite. She hadn't been satisfied until she had tried on every dress and every pair of shoes in her size. The tailored clothes Roxey had selected for her didn't impress the child in the least. The more ruffles and lace a dress boasted, the better. As a result, they'd spent hours combing the shops for just the right dress for Cissy. If it had been up to her, Roxey would have grabbed the first one that fit, then joined Seth and Brandon at the game. Stuffing herself with hot dogs and watching the Louisville Redbirds play baseball was a heck of a lot more fun than flipping through racks of dresses. But Cissy had asked to go shopping and shopping was what they would do.

Even though they were the last shoppers to leave Oxmoor Mall, Roxey and Cissy still beat Seth and Brandon home. Since they had time on their hands, Cissy begged Roxey to allow her to try on her new outfit.

Cissy caught the hem of her dress in her fingertips and spun around in a fast circle, the full skirt billowing out from her skinny legs. "Don't you think I look just like Cinderella?"

Roxey sat down on the edge of her bed and smiled. "You could be her twin."

"And you could be the fairy godmother. You couldn't be the mean old stepmother. You're too nice."

Oblivious to the fact that Roxey's breath had caught in her throat, Cissy skipped to the cheval mirror to check her reflection.

Stepmother? Just hearing the word shook Roxey to the core. Her dreams for the past twenty-four hours hadn't included being a stepmother. Seth Dandridge's wife, yes. She'd definitely fantasized about that. But the reality that marrying Seth would entail being the mother to two children hadn't surfaced until just now.

She glanced at Cissy preening before the mirror. The frilly new dress, red patent leather shoes and lacy socks had transformed the waiflike child into a little princess, who at the moment was feeling very proud of her new image. It would be easy to mother Cissy, for the child welcomed any attention. But Brandon? A frown sliced across Roxey's face. Brandon would have a hard time accepting her as his stepmother. He was having a difficult enough time accepting her as his friend.

Roxey shook herself to clear the thoughts from her head. Why was she spending time worrying about something that hadn't even happened? For heaven's sake! Seth had never mentioned marriage!

"Cissy, come over here and let me straighten your hair ribbon."

"Do you think Daddy will like my new clothes?"

Roxey held the little girl at arm's length. "Well, of course he will. You look beautiful."

"When do I get to wear my new dress?"

"Tuesday we're having dinner with my parents. You can wear it then." Roxey paused and cocked her head, listening. "I think I hear your dad's truck. Change back into your play clothes so we can surprise him, okay?"

Cissy's shoulders sagged like a sail that had lost its wind. "Do I have to? I wanted Daddy to see me all dressed up."

"Yes, you have to. The ball isn't until Tuesday night, Cinderella! And you certainly don't want Prince Charming to see your dress before the ball." Anxious to get downstairs and see Seth, Roxey spun Cissy around and her fingers fairly flew down the length of tiny buttons on the back of the new dress. With a light swat to Cissy's behind, she sent the child on her way. "I'll be downstairs on the patio. Come down when you finish changing."

The saddest little voice called back, "O-o-ka-a-ay."

Roxey couldn't help smiling as she hurried down the stairs. She hadn't realized how much the new dress meant to Cissy. Or maybe it was how the new dress made Cissy feel. At any rate, it was best to save it until the dinner party.

As Roxey approached the kitchen, she could hear Brandon's excited voice. "And when Pete hit that grounder to center field, forcing the guy on second to slide into third—man, what a play!"

Seth was leaning against the counter top with his long legs crossed lazily at the ankles, watching Brandon pace back and forth across the length of the kitchen.

"Hi, guys!" Roxey walked to Seth's side and slipped her arm through his, giving it a slight squeeze. "Sounds like you two had a good time."

Brandon's smile quickly disappeared and his voice became sullen. "It was okay." He turned his back to them and looked out the patio door to the pool.

Now what had she done wrong? Deciding to ignore the boy's moodiness, Roxey turned to Seth with a smile. "I'm cooking hamburgers on the grill tonight. Would y'all like to swim while they're grilling?"

"Sounds good to me. How about you, Brandon?"

Brandon remained with his back to them and pushed up one shoulder in a disinterested shrug.

Roxey felt the brunt of Brandon's animosity. She glanced up at Seth and saw him frowning at his son's back. Before he could voice his displeasure at Brandon's rudeness, Roxey pulled away from Seth and began to pull out items from the refrigerator needed for the cookout. "You two go on upstairs and change your clothes, and while you're up there, tell Cissy to put on her swimsuit."

Seth squatted beside her in front of the refrigerator, purposefully brushing his knee against her thigh. "Want me to stay and help?"

As she turned to face him, ready to accept his offer, Roxey noticed Brandon had twisted his head around and was frowning at his dad. She quickly changed her mind. "No, that's okay. Go ahead with Brandon and change. This won't take a minute for me to organize."

She saw Seth's disappointed look at her refusal, but it couldn't be helped. Obviously Brandon felt threatened by her friendship with his father, and she certainly didn't want to add to his moodiness.

By the time Seth and the children reached the patio, Roxey had the grill going and was sitting in a chair beside the pool. The children headed straight for the water, but Seth sat down beside her and draped an arm across the back of her chair.

The weight and warmth of his arm against her neck brought tingles of pleasure shooting down her spine. She tipped back her head and smiled at him. For a moment, she wished the children weren't with them and they could freely touch without fear of upsetting anyone.

As if he knew her thoughts, his face took on a wistful look, and he squeezed the back of her neck with his fingers. "This is really nice, Roxey. I can't remember the last time I did something with the kids that didn't in some way revolve around work."

"I'm glad. Everyone needs to get away from work occasionally. Even when it's work they love." She glanced at the pool where the children played in the shallow end. "Who's minding the farm while you're all here?"

"Miss Bertha's brother came up to stay with her, and he and a high school kid who helps me out part-time are taking care of things."

"And I'll bet you're worried sick everything will fall apart while you're away."

Seth cocked his head to the side to look at her. "You don't think I know how to relax and have a good time, do you?"

She chuckled at his defensive demeanor. "To be honest, no."

He leaned closer, a mischievous smile sparking his dark eyes. "Well, let me tell you something, little lady. You have a lot to learn about this old boy. Fun is my middle name." Without any warning, he scooped her out of the chair and into his arms.

Taken by surprise, Roxey was at first motionless, but when he stood and started walking toward the edge of the pool, she wrapped her arms around his neck and hung on for dear life. "Oh, please, Seth. Don't. You know I hate to get my hair wet."

"So I've heard." He stepped a little closer, his smile evidenced by the sparkle of white teeth showing just beneath his mustache.

She tightened her grip on his neck. "I swear to you, Seth—*Fun*—Dandridge, if you throw me in, I'm taking you with me."

He faked an appalled look. "You wouldn't dare."

"Oh, yes, I would."

"Well, then start taking, lady, 'cause here you go." He swung her back, but as his arms arced forward to pitch her in, instead of releasing her, he let out a war whoop and allowed the momentum of the swing to carry them both into the pool, Roxey still in his arms. They hit the water simultaneously with Roxey's scream swallowed up by the clear blue depths.

Taking advantage of the momentary privacy the water offered, Seth held her close against him, his lips seeking hers to steal a quick kiss before their buoyancy forced them upward.

When Roxey and Seth broke through the surface, Brandon and Cissy were both standing in the shallow end staring bug-eyed at their father and Roxey, who were laughing and sputtering as they clung to each other. Seth called out to them, "What's wrong with you kids? Haven't you ever seen anyone having a good time before?"

Brandon and Cissy turned to look at each other, then shrugged their shoulders and turned away, obviously convinced their dad had finally lost his mind.

Roxey had planned her week carefully, trying to balance fun outings with educational ones. Most of the things she'd arranged were based on activities that included the children—with the exception of Tuesday afternoon. Tuesday was the day Roxey had set aside to prove to Seth that Cissy would be better off in a special school.

Traffic rushed by them in a blur as Roxey drove slowly down the Watterson Expressway, bargaining for time in which to persuade Seth to at least visit the Dyslexic School.

She stole a glance at him. Wearing a pout that would rival that of a two-year-old, he sat opposite her, glaring out the side window. His demeanor was enough to cow Roxey into turning the car around and going back to her house. But she had made this appointment for Cissy's sake, and Cissy deserved a chance.

"Look at it this way, Seth. You aren't committing yourself to anything. You're merely investigating all your options. And when will you have a day available to do this again?"

Puckering his lips out in a frown, Seth harrumphed. Women! Always conniving and sneaking around. He should have sensed a trap when Roxey so conveniently arranged for Cissy and Brandon to play with her cousin's children, then nonchalantly asked if he would like to take a drive. The only thing that kept him from demanding she turn the car around and take him home was the fact that she'd been such a good sport when she was at the farm. She'd even helped with chores, which certainly hadn't been part of their agreement. And it was true he'd never have an opportunity like this again to visit the school.

With a deep sigh of resignation, he capitulated. "Probably never." He sat up straighter in the seat and offered Roxey a halfhearted smile. "Okay. I'll go. But only to look mind you."

When they arrived at the school, Roxey felt an immediate if imperceptible tenseness in Seth. As they toured the classrooms and buildings, the tension built and he became more and more withdrawn, until by the time they reached the counselor's office he was as impassive as a wooden Indian.

"How old is your daughter, Mr. Dandridge?"

Roxey waited for Seth to respond to the counselor's question, but when it became obvious he didn't intend to, she quickly said, "Cissy is six."

Roxey asked questions, and responded to the counselor's inquiries about Cissy to the best of her knowledge. At one point, Roxey glanced in Seth's direction and was surprised to see his face was flushed with anger.

It wasn't until they were back in the car and on the way to her house that she drew enough courage to look at him again. He sat rigid, his palms cupped on his knees while he glared at the windshield.

She forced a cheery note to her voice. "Well, what did you think?"

He crossed his arms like a shield across his chest and let her words bounce off him, refusing to even acknowledge her question. He'd always felt he had a grasp on his children's problems, and found the necessary solutions to them. Now Roxey was throwing new solutions at him. Solutions he was having a hard time accepting. He was losing control of the situation, and he didn't like it one bit.

"The theory supporting their curriculum impressed me. How about you?"

When he continued to ignore her, Roxey's own temper snapped and she whipped the car to the shoulder of the road, stomped on the brake and threw the gear shift into park. Twisting around in the seat, she demanded, "Talk to me, Seth. Tell me what you're thinking."

He spun to face her, his face tight with anger. "Talk to you! I'm surprised you even care what I think. You're so damn busy making decisions and trying to run our lives."

Roxey's jaw dropped open. "I am *not* trying to run your lives! I'm only trying to help you make the best decision for your children."

"And who asked for your help?" he demanded before jabbing his index finger back at his chest. "*I* sure as hell didn't!"

Tears welled in Roxey's eyes at the suddenness of his attack. She hadn't meant to interfere. She'd only wanted to help. But maybe she had overstepped her bounds.

Forcing her voice to remain calm, she attempted to justify her actions. "When I agreed to spend a week on your farm, allowing you the opportunity to convince me you were qualified to teach your children, it was with the stipulation that you would spend a week in the city so I could prove home schooling might not be the best choice for your children. The visit to the Dyslexia School was intended to show you options, *not* an attempt to run your life."

"What if sending her to this school upsets Cissy?" Seth snapped back. "God knows she's experienced enough rejection in her life. First her mother, then the kids at school because she was different."

"But don't you see? This school can help her overcome that difference."

Dark, angry eyes continued to bore into her blue ones, but Roxey refused to look away. She was convinced the Dyslexia School was the answer for Cissy. But when she noticed the shimmer in Seth's eyes before he turned away, Roxey quickly forgot her anger and leaned to touch a hand to his sleeve.

"Seth?"

He jerked his arm from her grasp and continued to stare through the side window, clamping his teeth so tight together a muscle ticed in his jaw. When he spoke, his voice was low and husky, almost a whisper. "She's my baby, Rox. How can I send my baby away to school?"

The desperation and pain in his voice cut Roxey to the core. In a flash she understood his anger as a guise to cover up a father's protective love for his child. She draped an arm across his broad shoulders. "Oh, Seth. I'm sorry. I didn't realize."

He leaned forward, propping his elbows on his knees and digging the heels of his hands into his eyes. Roxey rubbed his back in soothing circles.

"It isn't necessary for Cissy to live at the school, Seth. It's only a thirty-minute drive. You can bring her to Louisville, drop her off, then come back in the afternoon to pick her up."

He cocked his head to look at her. "Think about what you're suggesting, Roxey. It'd be an hour both ways, five days a week. I'm a farmer. I get up at daybreak and work till dusk. There isn't time in my schedule to be running a shuttle to Louisville every day."

He leaned back against the leather seat and took her hand, pulling it to his lap and running his fingers between hers in a distracted way. "I agree the school would be the best thing for her, but I can't do it. Not physically, and not emotionally. She's my baby, Roxey. It's that simple."

"I'm not trying to argue with you, but if you don't have time to drive her, how will you ever find the time to teach her?"

A weak attempt at a smile pushed up one corner of his mouth. "There aren't any rules as to what time or what days I teach her at home. In the winter months, the sun sets early, so I'll have more time in the evenings to work with her." He turned to her, the look in his eyes begging for understanding. "I love my kids, Roxey. They'll always get the best I can give them. You believe that, don't you?"

Roxey wrapped her arms around his neck and buried her face in the crook of his shoulder. "Yes, Seth, I believe you."

"Oh, Miss Classen! You look beautiful." Cissy sounded awestruck.

Roxey turned and glanced in the mirror again. She looked the same to herself as she always did. An invitation for dinner at her parents' home always required dressing up, and tonight was special because she was introducing Seth and his children to her parents. But she didn't understand Cissy's attitude toward the dress—it wasn't even new. In fact, she'd worn it several times before and no one had ever commented on it.

Maybe the dress was a little too risqué. She turned around and looked over her shoulder at the back of her dress. The cowl neckline, which touched the deep hollow of her throat in the front, scooped low in the back, exposing bare skin almost to her waist. No, she thought with a quick shake of her head. The dress was tastefully designed and she'd never once had any qualms about wearing it.

She turned to the mirror again and leaned in to examine her face. There *was* something different about her. Something she couldn't quite put her finger on. She lightly touched her face. Maybe it was her cheeks. They had a little more color than usual, but that was probably a result of all the sun she'd been getting. And there might be a little more sparkle to her eyes.... Oh, good heavens! She was allowing all Cissy's talk about Cinderella and fairy godmothers to infect her with a sense of magic, too.

"Come on, Cissy. Our coach awaits us."

Cissy covered her mouth with her hand as she giggled. "Will it change into a pumpkin at midnight?"

With one hand pressed lightly at the child's back, Roxey guided Cissy out of the bedroom and down the stairs. "If it does, I'm suing."

From the foot of the stairway, Seth heard their laughter and turned to watch them descend the stairs. The sight the two of them created melted the smile from his face and left his lower jaw hanging slack. On the farm, Roxey had worn jeans and shorts, and though her clothes contained designer labels and looked great on her, they hadn't prepared him for this. She looked like an angel floating down the stairs, the skirt of her dress swirling around her legs like a blue cloud.

"How do we look, Daddy?"

The voice pulled his gaze from Roxey to the small child at her side. He knelt almost reverently in front of Cissy and touched a tentative finger to the blond curls swirling to her shoulders. "And who is this pretty little girl?"

"Oh, Daddy. It's me. Cissy."

He glanced down at the frilly little dress, the lacy socks and the shiny red shoes and had to swallow back the lump building in his throat. His baby girl looked so grown-up and every bit the lady. Seeing her dressed this way made him feel guilty for not realizing girls sometimes needed more than blue jeans and sneakers.

On a deep sigh so filled with regret and love that he felt a tangible pain on its release, he took her little hand in his. "So it is. I hardly recognized you. You look beautiful, Cissy."

"This is the new dress Miss Classen helped me pick out, and she fixed my hair and everything. Don't you think Miss Classen looks pretty, too?"

Seth glanced up at Roxey and warmed her with his smile before returning his gaze to Cissy's. "Every bit as pretty as you."

Cissy fingered the lapel of Seth's jacket. "You look pretty, too, Daddy. Except . . ." She placed a finger to the corner of her mouth and frowned as she studied him. "I think you're too fuzzy."

"What?" he choked out with a laugh.

"You're too fuzzy. Miss Classen trimmed my hair, maybe she'd trim yours, too."

He glanced up at Roxey. "What do you think, Miss Classen? Have you got time for another haircut before we go?"

With a quick glance at her wristwatch, Roxey shrugged. "I guess. But I've never cut a man's hair before."

Seth stood. "Well, I guess there's always a first time. Brandon's in the den watching television, Cissy. Why don't you join him? We'll holler when we're through playing barbershop."

Roxey led the way to her dressing room, and after settling Seth on a stool, stood behind him with the scissors poised at his ear level. She chewed nervously on her bottom lip. "Are you sure you want me to do this?"

He smiled at her nervous reflection in the vanity mirror. "Yes, I'm sure."

"You won't lose all your strength like Samson or anything, will you?"

A deep chuckle shook his chest. "No."

She rested the heel of her hands against his shoulders and looked at him in the mirror. "Maybe you'd better take off your shirt so we won't get hair all over it."

He waggled his eyebrows at her as he began to work the buttons free. "This could get interesting."

It was a mistake. As soon as the first three buttons were freed, exposing his chest, Roxey knew she shouldn't have asked him to remove it. Dark hair curled and swirled across the breadth of his chest and when he reached his arms behind him to allow the shirt to fall free, squared pads of muscles formed, making Roxey's breath catch in her throat as memories of the afternoon they'd shared together in this very room surged through her, awakening prickling points of desire throughout her body.

Grabbing a towel from the brass rack, she quickly draped it across his shoulders, covering a large portion of his back and chest. Her fingers shook slightly as she picked up the scissors again.

Seth caught the hand holding the scissors by the wrist and twisted Roxey around until she landed on his lap with a slight plop. His lips closed over hers, silencing her startled exclamation. He deepened the kiss until gradually he felt the tension ease from her body.

"I've been wanting to do that all day." He nibbled little teasing kisses against her throat.

The towel had slipped off his shoulders, and Roxey did what she'd wanted to earlier...she twined her fingers through the dark hair on his chest. Breathless, she replied, "Me, too."

He turned his head to nibble behind her ear. "Shouldn't you be cutting my hair?"

Her eyes closed against the intoxicating feel of his lips. "What hair?" she whispered. She felt the rumble of his chuckle through her fingers pressed against his chest.

"The hair Cissy will be expecting to be trimmed."

Roxey sat up straight on his lap and faced him, her lips almost level with his. "Oh, yeah." She touched her fingers to his beard and with a smile lifted her gaze to his. "If we start with your beard, I won't have to move, I can stay right here on your lap."

Cupping her buttocks in his hands and scooting her closer against him, he replied in a husky voice, "Sounds good to me."

Nine

The haircut took much longer than expected. Roxey teasingly blamed the delay on Seth, saying that he'd purposely distracted her, while Seth blamed Roxey for being a distraction. They reached the Classen estate just in time to be seated for dinner in the formal dining room of her parents' home.

Each prism of the multitiered Waterford chandelier shimmered like diamonds on a princess's tiara, complementing the stems of crystal at each of ten place settings. Irish linen covered the table and a matching napkin shaped into a fan rested in the center of each of the Wedgewood china dinner plates. Two heavily carved sterling silver candelabras, each holding twelve tapered candles, flanked a leaded crystal vase of fresh-cut flowers.

Roxey nervously chewed at her bottom lip as she noted each detail of the room. She tried to put herself in Seth's place and imagine how she would feel if she were seeing the Classen estate for the first time. Her shoulders drooped as she decided it was impossible. She'd grown up in this house and couldn't imagine it any way but the way it was: heavy with priceless antiques and even heavier with family traditions. But how did it appear to others? Especially Seth.

Silver and crystal gleamed everywhere she looked, reflecting a distorted image of Roxey like the mirrors in a fun house. Fat and squatty, tall and pencil thin.

The images seemed to tease Roxey, laughing at her as they loomed indistinct and perverted. Other things around her, things she had seen all her life, appeared different when pictured through the wrong medium. A niggling of fear began to eat away at what remained of her self-confidence. How did Seth see her when surrounded by the opulence of her parents' home? Did she appear as the same person he'd gotten to know on the farm? Or even the same person he'd made love to at her town house?

In frustration Roxey looked away. Seth would draw his own conclusions about her and her family and there was nothing she could do to change them.

As always, Harriet Classen, Roxey's mother, had selected her dinner guests carefully and, with the skill and cunning of a military field marshal, had strategically seated them around the table. To her left she had placed Seth Dandridge. On her right, her Uncle Lionel, who at times could be as boring as yesterday's leftovers. At the opposite end of the long table, Roxey sat at her father's left, and beside her—thanks to her mother's clever placement of name cards—sat Miles Harrison, Louisville's most eligible bachelor.

If only her mother had seated Seth next to Roxey, she would have felt better about the situation. But as it was, she worried about him, wondering how he was faring with the indomitable Harriet Classen on one side and Roxey's sister, Monica, on the other. Would he feel out of place? Awkward? She frowned as she watched Monica lean close to him, her full breasts brushing against his sleeve as she whispered something in his ear.

Long-stemmed roses interlaced with greenery and stalks of lilac dominated the center of the table, blocking Roxey's view of Seth's reaction to her sister. She quickly added to her growing list of worries as she nervously watched her sister, a three-time loser and obviously on the prowl for husband number four.

Roxey scooted her chair closer to her father's and strained to peek around the bank of flowers in time to see her mother had diverted Seth's attention away from Monica. With a childish pout, Monica sank back against her chair and sipped her wine. Accustomed to her older sister's sulkiness, Roxey ignored her and looked again at Seth.

It was rude to stare, but Roxey couldn't help it. Was it the haircut? The crisp white shirt and tie? Or maybe the sport coat? No, she decided, the attraction she felt couldn't be attributed to any outer qualities. It was something within him. Perhaps the tenderness he fought so hard to hide or the gentleness difficult to ascribe to so large a man.

In the flickering candlelight, she watched him ease a finger behind the stiff white collar of his starched shirt and felt a pang of guilt. Not once had he complained about coming here. He hadn't even protested when she'd told him he would have to wear a coat and tie. She watched him arch his neck up and away, then release the collar in defeat. Not a suit-and-tie man, that much was sure. And although he looked handsome all dressed up, Roxey realized she preferred him in his chambray shirt and jeans.

Then, as if he felt Roxey's gaze, Seth turned to her with a soft smile and winked. A warmth quickly spread through Roxey.

"Is this Dandridge guy a friend of yours?"

With regret, Roxey shifted her attention from Seth to Miles. "Yes. We met a few weeks ago." She picked up her wineglass and took a sip.

"I haven't seen you at the club lately. Are you still playing tennis?"

Roxey shrugged. "Some. I really haven't had time since I started working."

Miles's tone was cocksure as he stretched an arm behind Roxey's chair and leaned close with a most engaging smile.

"Well, we'll have to change that. How about a game to-morrow?"

From the opposite end of the table, Seth watched Miles and Roxey. Jealousy wasn't an emotion Seth was accustomed to experiencing, but as he watched Miles Harrison laying on the charm for Roxey, a slow anger began to burn just beneath the surface. Miles was the classic rich kid. Everything about him screamed Ivy League, from his razor-cut blond hair, to his argyle socks.

"Don't they make a handsome couple?" Monica's honey-eyed voice echoed the very truth Seth was fighting to deny.

He turned to her with what he hoped was an expression devoid of emotion. "Who?"

She laughed gaily and lightly pushed at his shoulder with a long manicured nail. "Why, Roxey and Miles, you silly boy. They were quite an item until Roxey took this job with the state." Monica glanced at Miles, then back to Seth. She allowed her gaze to sweep slowly down Seth's upper body, then batted her eyelashes seductively at him. "Personally, I prefer a more mature and experienced man. How about you, Seth?" She made a slow journey around her mouth with the tip of her tongue. "How do you like your women?"

"Daddy!" Cissy whispered loudly from the other side of Monica. "I need to use the rest room."

Monica gave Cissy a withering look before turning to Seth with a sugary smile. "I'll take her. Come on, honey," she said to Cissy as she caught the child's upper arm a little too tightly with her long, tapered fingers.

While Monica and Cissy excused themselves from the table, Seth rose, then sat back down, relieved to be free of Monica's smothering attentiveness, if even for a few minutes.

But his reprieve was short-lived. Harriet turned to him with a five-dollar smile that didn't quite reach her eyes.

"Roxey tells us you own a farm, Mr. Dandridge."

"Yes, ma'am, I do."

"How fascinating. What crops do you grow?"

"Well, for the time being, only hay to feed my cattle in the winter months and enough vegetables to feed us."

"Oh, so you're a rancher then."

"No. I'm a farmer. Since I'm doing most of the work myself, it's taking me a while to clear the land and prepare the fields for crops. I'll be growing tobacco eventually, but I plan to keep a small herd of cattle as well."

"Roxey mentioned that you were once employed here in Louisville."

"Yes, ma'am. I served as a vice president of a corporation whose home offices are located here."

"Whatever possessed you to leave such a position to become a farmer?"

She said *farmer* as if it was a four-letter word, and as if saying the word soiled her hands. This riled Seth, but for Roxey's sake he didn't allow the anger to show. His voice remained calm, but his fingers tightened on the stem of the wineglass in his hand.

"Farming is something I enjoy. Owning my own land, being my own boss, doing an honest day's work without destroying someone else in the process—that's something I couldn't achieve working in the city."

"Are you saying blue-collar jobs are preferable to white-collar ones?"

"For me they are."

"What do you think, Uncle Lionel?" Harriet turned to the elderly man on her left.

Uncle Lionel hadn't said more than three words during the entire evening. His sole achievement had been in spooning every drop of soup from his bowl and every smidgen of salad from his plate. "Think about what, Harriet?"

"Blue-collar jobs versus white-collar ones."

Monica returned with Cissy in time to hear the question Harriet directed to Uncle Lionel and muttered under her breath. "Oh, God. Be prepared. This could take a while."

Her prediction proved true. Uncle Lionel expounded on the advantages of being a professional man over those of being a farmer, then reversed his thinking and extolled the virtues of being a farmer over those of having a white-collar job. Between bites of buttered croissants, crown pork roast and tender steamed asparagus he droned on and on, totally unaware everyone around him had grown glassy eyed and had stopped listening long ago.

By the time Harriet suggested they retire to the living room for coffee, Seth felt as if he'd been beaten up and left for dead. What with defending his chosen life-style, listening to Uncle Lionel's mindless prattle and fending off Monica's libidinous advances, Seth was exhausted.

As the group drifted across the massive entry hall to the formal living room, Seth hesitated at the base of the curving staircase. Portraits hung along the wall leading up to the second floor. From their lofty perch, several generations of Classens looked down at him, their faces stern, as if they, too, were judging him.

Judging him? The thought caught him unaware. But, yes, he *did* feel as if Roxey's parents were judging him. And after the lengthy discussion with Harriet Classen during dinner, he suspected he hadn't measured up to her standards.

As he stood at the base of the marble staircase, he thought of his home with its polished wood floors and rough-hewn log walls, comparing it to the Italian marble beneath his feet and the walls of raw silk surrounding him. When he first met Roxey, Seth had built a fortress around his heart in order to protect himself from what he knew he had no business being attracted to. Roxey had slowly and methodically knocked down those walls brick by brick until she'd won his acceptance of her. But now, being in her parents' home and confronted with the life-style she was accustomed to, he felt all the old defensiveness return.

He sensed someone behind him and knew without turning it was Roxey. Electrical currents flowed between them, charging the air, and when her fingers touched his back, he felt a keen resurgence of energy. She moved around him and stepped up onto the first marble stair, putting herself almost at eye level with him. With an understanding smile, she reached up and slipped her fingers around the knot of his tie and pulled it loose, then unbuttoned the top button of his shirt.

"There," she said with a deep sigh of relief, as if the tight collar had been choking her as well. "That's better."

Something about the action—whether its intimacy or possibly the fact it symbolized Roxey's difference from her staid family—made Seth's doubts fade back out of sight.

He touched a finger lightly to her cheek, then slipped his hand to cup her neck. Roxey's lips parted expectantly, and he found he couldn't resist. With a quick glance to ensure they were alone, he touched his lips to hers, tentatively at first, then pressing deeper, searching for the answer to a question he dared not ask.

There was a loud gasp from the doorway at their left. They quickly released each other and turned to see the shocked face of Harriet Classen.

With her chin lifted unnaturally high and her hands clasped tightly at her waist, she gave them both a condemning look. "Roxanne. Perhaps you and your guest should join us in the living room for coffee."

It took only a moment for the surprise at being caught kissing to wear off and the anger to set in. Roxey offered her mother a tight smile. "Yes, Mother."

With an apologetic look at Seth, Roxey led him across the hall to the living room. Persian rugs of varied sizes and shapes covered the polished hardwood floors of the Classens' formal living room, discreetly segmenting the room into conversation areas filled with Louis XIV sofas and Queen Anne chairs. When Roxey and Seth entered the room, the other guests were scattered about in loose groups, talking and sipping coffee from thin china cups.

Immediately, Monica was there, pulling Seth away from Roxey. "You naughty boy! Where have you been? I want to ask your opinion about something. I've been thinking about investing in some land and don't know the first thing about it. Would you . . ."

Monica's voice faded as Roxey watched her lead Seth away. After years of losing the attention of first boys, then men to her older sister's feminine wiles, Roxey supposed she should be accustomed to it, but she wasn't.

Finding herself on her own, she glanced around the room. Brandon was sitting on a sofa reading a book. Cissy sat beside him, swinging her feet, her hands clasped between her knees. In front of the sofa was a round glass coffee table perched on a heavy brass frame of Oriental design. Clustered on the tabletop was a collection of Meissen porcelain boxes. Cissy spied the miniature boxes and knelt at the table to examine them more closely.

Roxey watched as Cissy picked up one of the priceless pieces and turned it around and around in her hand to examine it, her eyes growing large in wonder. With her gaze fixed on the box in her hand, Cissy stood, glanced up and saw Roxey and started to walk toward her. But just before she reached her, the child's toe caught on the fringed edge of a Persian rug, and she tripped, landing on the floor with a thud and sending the box flying across the room.

The porcelain box hit the hardwood floor with a shattering sound, shooting pieces of porcelain in every direction. A hush fell over the room as every eye turned to look first at the fragmented box, then at the pale and stricken Cissy.

Unfortunately, Harriet moved first. "Oh, my word! My Meissen collection!" She hurried over and began to pick up the useless pieces.

"I'm s-s-orry. I didn't mean to b-break it." Huge tears rolled down Cissy's face.

Harriet ignored the child's distress and continued to gather up the shards of porcelain.

Her mother's insensitive treatment of Cissy mobilized Roxey. "Of course you didn't," Roxey soothed as she knelt to pull Cissy into her arms. "It was an accident. Are you hurt? Did you cut yourself?"

Cissy managed to shake her head before throwing her arms around Roxey and burying her face against her friend's chest. Gulping sobs shook the small child's shoulders while Roxey continued to soothe her.

Suddenly Seth was beside them, pulling Cissy from Roxey's arms and cradling the child protectively against his chest. He whispered against Cissy's soft hair, "It's okay, baby, Daddy's got you." He turned slightly to Roxey. "Perhaps it would be best if we left now." He motioned for Brandon, who sat frozen on the sofa, to join him. "Let's go, son."

His eyes dark, and his face taut with carefully controlled emotion, Seth walked to Roxey's father and extended his hand to him. "I'm terribly sorry about the damage, sir. I realize the box is irreplaceable, but if you'll notify me of the cost, I'll gladly pay for it." He withdrew his hand and stepped back, and with a nod that took in the whole room said, "Thank you for your hospitality. If you'll excuse us."

Harriet at least had the good grace to look embarrassed. "I'm sorry, perhaps I've overreacted. Our insurance will cover the breakage. You needn't worry." She gave a nervous laugh. "Tomorrow I'm sure we won't even remember this happened."

Seth's expression never wavered as he glanced from Harriet to Cissy, then back to Harriet.

"You may not, but something tells me Cissy will never forget."

Nor would Roxey. Later that night after they'd returned home, and while Seth put the children to bed, Roxey slipped out to her patio. She sat on one of the wrought-iron chairs with her knees tucked beneath her chin. A soft breeze whispered through the trees, carrying with it the sweet smell of rain.

Lightning flashed across the blue-black sky in jagged streaks, and seconds later the sound of thunder reverberated through Roxey as it rumbled across the night.

Grandmother Classen had always loved summer storms, and it was she who had taught Roxey to love them. One night after finding Roxey cowering under her bed during a storm, her grandmother Classen had taken the child outside to sit on the porch. Making a game of it, she taught Roxey the mystery and beauty of nature's more volatile side. They took turns guessing where the next lightning would strike and counted the seconds that elapsed before the thunder clapped. Grandmother had told her there was nothing to fear in thunder, because it was only the sound of the angels rolling bowling balls through the heavens.

Memories of Grandmother Classen brought a new wave of tears to Roxey's eyes. She had always been her grandmother's favorite. Born a few generations too soon, Elizabeth Classen had never been allowed to use her keen business mind—at least not publicly—and as a result, when she recognized that same perceptiveness in Roxey, she had encouraged her granddaughter to pursue a career. Grandmother died two years before Roxey graduated from college, but Roxey sensed her grandmother's pride in her accomplishments.

Her grandmother's wisdom had extended beyond just good business sense. Roxey's lip trembled as she wished fervently her grandmother were still alive and had been there for dinner tonight. Grandmother Classen wouldn't have made such a scene over the Meissen box. Roxey knew that because she remembered once breaking a Lladro figurine. When her mother screamed at her, Grandmother had come to Roxey's defense, telling Harriet that no possession was as fragile as a child's feelings, nor as priceless as a child's self-esteem.

Roxey hadn't thought about that incident in years. At the time, she hadn't understood her grandmother's softly spoken reprimand to Harriet, but now she did. She wrapped her arms beneath her knees and pulled them tighter against her chest. Ordinarily, she loved to sit outside and watch summer storms, but not tonight. The tension in the air warred with the tension within her body, stretching her nerves even tighter.

It was all her fault. If she hadn't invited Seth and the children to go with her to her parents' home… If she hadn't been so stubborn and insisted on Seth bringing the children to Louisville so she could prove him wrong about home schooling... If she hadn't denied Seth the right to teach his children at home in the first place... If, if, if. Her head ached with all the ifs.

Seth was a good father. He'd proved that within twenty-four hours of her arrival at his farm. The decisions he made for the children were made with Cissy's and Brandon's best interests at heart. Roxey saw that now.

Then why didn't she just go inside and tell him he had her approval to teach his kids at home and send them on their way? Her chin lifted defiantly. Because she still firmly believed Cissy and Brandon needed the opportunity to interact with children their own age. The trembling of her lip and the deep ache in the region of her heart told her she wasn't being totally honest.

No. It wasn't just the children. Roxey was afraid. Afraid that if she let him go she might never see him again.

She heard the shushing sound of the patio door sliding open and quickly sat up and wiped the trace of tears from her eyes. When she turned, Seth stood not more than five feet away, looking up at the clouds scudding across the sky that occasionally blocked out the moon's light.

"Looks like we're in for a storm." His voice sounded loud, yet distant in the darkness.

"Yes." Roxey sniffed and gestured to a chair. "Have a seat."

As he pulled the chair closer to hers, lightning lit the night like rockets on the Fourth of July. Silently, Roxey counted as she had so many times before with Grandmother Classen. One, two, three, four, five... When she reached ten, thunder rumbled in the distance, a little closer this time, a little louder than the time before.

The wind kicked up and turned the waves on the pool into miniature whitecaps that lapped against the blue-tiled sides. Roxey lifted her face to the wind and felt her skin tighten as the salty tears dried on her cheeks. As if he sensed her need for solitude, Seth remained quiet, but caught her hand in his and squeezed it in reassurance.

The unexpectedness of the gesture caught Roxey by surprise. The tenderness of it squeezed at her heart, and she swallowed back the emotion building in her throat.

"I'm sorry for my family's behavior, Seth. I—"

"Don't, Roxey. I don't blame you." He dropped her hand and leaned forward, gripping his hands together as he rested his elbows against his knees. "And I don't blame your family, either. I should have known better. That house is no place for kids."

"But Mother acted—"

"Please don't blame your mother. I don't want to cause ill will between you and your family." He stood and strode to the edge of the pool. With his arms folded across his chest, he stared at the dark water as if within its depths he could find the answers to all his problems.

Suddenly, he turned to her. "I think it would be best if the kids and I left tomorrow."

Moisture welled in Roxey's eyes and burned her nostrils. Leave? Oh, God, please. Not yet. She'd only begun to realize how much she needed him, how much she wanted to be a part of his and his children's lives.

She wanted to beg him not to go, she wanted to tell him she loved him and needed him, but her pride held her back. Grasping at every bit of inner strength she possessed, she held back the flood of tears that raged for release. "If you think that's best." She stood, too, and not trusting herself to look at him, looked at the sky, then at her fingers templed at waist level.

"I've been thinking about your application, and I may have come up with a compromise."

She felt his gaze upon her, expectant and questioning, but remained with her gaze cast downward. "If you promise to enroll Cissy and Brandon in extracurricular activities, I'll approve your application to give the children home schooling."

Silence lay heavy between them for what seemed to Roxey an inordinate length of time. She squeezed her eyes shut and turned to walk back to the house. His voice stopped her.

"I thank you for that, Roxey."

With her back still to him, she replied, "There's no need for thanks." She heard the break in her voice and, not trusting herself to say more, hurried into the house, closing the door behind her and behind the heartrending sob she could no longer suppress.

Seth knew she was crying and he hated himself for it. Yet it was better this way. Roxey's life-style was so different from the one he'd chosen for himself and his kids. The visit to her family's home had shown him that. He couldn't afford to buy her the things she was accustomed to—not with what he made farming. In the past, when he'd been on his way to the top, he might eventually have earned that much, but not now. And he was too old and too stubborn to start over again. Which brought to mind another reason to end this relationship. Roxey was so young. Twelve years lay like a gaping cavern between them, waiting for him to attempt to close the breach, waiting for him to slip in so it could swallow him up. For the past three weeks, he'd allowed himself to act and feel like some young bull, but right now he felt every one of his thirty-six years. Roxey deserved someone her own age. Someone who didn't come with a ready-made family. Someone who could offer her a life like the one she was accustomed to. Someone like...Miles Harrison.

The name whispered across his lips, and like a benediction from heaven, lightning streaked across the sky, followed immediately by a deafening clap of thunder. Raindrops began to fall, slowly at first, then faster, stinging Seth's uplifted face and camouflaging his tears.

Yes, it was better this way. But it didn't ease the hurt any.

Ten

___

From the bay window of her parents' sun room, Roxey watched a squirrel scamper across the yellowed grass with a pecan clamped securely between his teeth. When had the season changed? Deep furrows creased her forehead as she concentrated hard, trying to recall when last she'd noticed the lawn being that rich blue-green, the color so unique to Kentucky bluegrass. Her shoulders sagged and the creases on her forehead smoothed as she gave up in frustration. It was no use. The past six weeks were a blur. She'd been living her life like an automaton, eating, sleeping, working—all without any conscious effort on her part.

The squirrel scurried up the trunk of the magnolia tree at the foot of the driveway and disappeared among the tree's waxy green foliage. A picture of another magnolia formed in her mind, one with a weathered swing hanging from its massive branches. Seth stood behind the swing, smiling, waiting, holding it steady for her. She squeezed her eyes shut and hugged her arms beneath her breasts, trying to block the image and suppress the pain these memories still brought her.

On a shuddery breath, she opened her eyes to a clear blue autumn sky. Even from within the house, she could sense the crispness in the air and smell the musky scent of decaying leaves.

The squirrel scampered back down the tree and across the yard. Winter was coming. Roxey's thoughts drifted again to Seth and his farm. What were he and the children doing today? The garden would be nearly empty now, the hay all baled and stacked in the barn. What did farmers do in the winter months?

Her hands flew to her temples and pressed as she squeezed her eyes shut. God! She had to stop this. Only three months had passed since she'd first met him, but almost six weeks without a word from him. It was time to accept the fact that Seth Dandridge was gone and get on with her life.

Suddenly it came to her. It was October. Nearly a year had passed since she'd taken the job with the state. She breathed in a deep cleansing breath, forcing her blue mood to recede. Before she met Seth, her goal had been to work at her father's bank. Somewhere along the way, that goal had lost importance. But now...

She squared her shoulders and turned purposefully for her father's study. No better time than the present to remind him of his promise to her.

"Jason! Are you listening to me?"

Harriet's shrill voice grated across Jason Classen's nerves. He carefully folded the *Wall Street Journal*, then pulled off his glasses as he leaned back in his chair. "Yes, Harriet, I heard you. You're concerned about Roxanne."

"Well, what are we going to do about it?"

"Do? What do you mean 'do'?"

"My word, Jason! Can't you see how serious this situation is? I saw that man kissing her. And ever since he and those children of his left, she's been moping around. What if she—" Her voice broke, and she delicately pressed a linen handkerchief to her lips. "What if she were to marry him?"

"Come now, Harriet. Roxey may be a bit rebellious, but—"

"What if it isn't rebellion? What if she thinks she really loves him?"

J.P. Classen became pensive, his brows drawn together and his lips slightly puckered. But before he could respond to his wife's rising hysteria, the door to his study pushed open.

"Am I interrupting anything?" Roxey breezed in and plopped down in the leather chair next to her mother and opposite her father's desk.

Harriet pasted on a sweet smile and leaned over to pat Roxey's arm. "Of course not, darling. Your father and I were just discussing our plans for the Thanksgiving holidays. What do you think of the three of us going on a cruise or perhaps a trip to Majorca?"

"Whatever." Roxey turned to her father, determined to convince him. "Dad, remember our deal? You said if I worked for a year outside the banking business, you'd give me a job at the bank?"

At his speculative nod, Roxey forged on. "Well, in two weeks I'll have worked for the state for twelve months. I love my work and I'll miss it, but I'm ready to move on. I want to work for you at the bank."

He remained thoughtful for a moment as he smoothed the folds of his newspaper. With a quick decisive gesture, he dropped the paper and leaned forward, resting his forearms on the desk top. "The timing on this may be fortuitous. We've just promoted one of our junior loan officers. Perhaps you could fill his position. In fact, come by first thing in the morning and we'll acquaint you with your duties."

"Can't tomorrow. I need to give the state two weeks notice."

Her father strained to conceal his impatience. "For heaven's sake, Roxanne. Surely you can—"

Roxey held up her hand as she interrupted him. "No, Dad. I owe them that much." She jumped up from her chair and hurried around the desk to give her father a quick hug. "Thanks, Dad. I promise you won't be sorry."

As soon as the door closed behind Roxanne, Harriet—who had remained unusually silent throughout the entire discussion—turned to her husband with a satisfied smile. "Jason, how clever you are. Perhaps now Roxanne will forget that awful man."

Seth walked through the silent house to the front hallway. His body ached with fatigue, yet sleep continued to evade him. As always, the night called him, drawing him to the porch, then on to the yard and the swing beneath the magnolia tree. Too many sleepless nights had been spent sitting on the weathered swing, drifting slowly back and forth with his elbows looped around the coarse ropes while memories of Roxey's laughter echoed through his mind.

He hesitated. Before him the front door loomed like a dark gaping hole, luring him to the outside. No. Not this time. It was time to put an end to the memories. Purposefully, he turned away from the door and strode into the living room. He snapped on the lamp on the end table before he flopped down on the sofa's deep cushions. He circled the room with his gaze.

He rarely entered this room. It always reminded him of Lorissa. She'd insisted they needed a formal living room and had furnished it with the formal furniture from their home in Louisville. He'd always thought that the off-white contemporary furniture had looked out of place in this house and had never fit in. Just like his ex-wife. Not that she'd even tried. He was glad she'd insisted upon taking the furniture with her when she left.

With so many other things needing his attention, it had taken Seth a while to replace the furniture. His attempts at interior decorating, he knew, were weak, but at least the things he'd purchased seemed more appropriate to a log cabin. His gaze fell on the coffee table. Magazines were scattered across its top. *Town and Country*, *Metropolitan Home*, *Harper's Bazaar*. Obviously Roxey had left them. Funny how even a few magazines seemed to give the room life, a warm lived-in feeling the room lacked before. He picked up one and began to thumb through it. Jewelry from Tiffany's and Gucci's. Clothes from Saks Fifth Avenue and Neiman-Marcus. Beautiful sleek women pictured with streamlined cars and handsome young men. Pictorial layouts of the rich and famous.

Anger and frustration built with each turn of the page until he finally slammed the magazine closed, stood and strode to the fireplace. He pulled a match from the tall brass box and scratched it across the rough brick wall. The match blazed, then shrunk to a steady flame. He touched the fire to the loose pages and held the magazine in his hand a moment while the flame caught and spread. When the heat became too intense, Seth tossed the burning reminder of Roxey into the fireplace.

So much for Roxanne Classen and her highfalutin magazines. Neither one belonged on his farm.

The young man sitting opposite Roxey in her office at the bank nervously clutched his cowboy hat while Roxey studied the sketches of barns and corrals and a sheet of tightly columned figures. She felt his gaze on her while she examined the layouts and double-checked his totals on her calculator.

The prospectus was rough and obviously prepared by the young man himself, but the hours spent preparing it were as obvious to Roxey as the man's belief in his dream.

"How long do you think it will be before you realize a profit, Mr. Jackson?"

"On the short side, a year. On the long…as much as two. But you have to understand, it takes a while to build good stock. I've already got ten good brood mares and one stud. All I need is another good stud and the additional barns and working pens to break the horses in."

Roxey frowned as she studied the figures before her. "The only collateral you have is a three-year-old truck and trailer worth approximately twelve thousand dollars, thirty acres of land that, because of its location, is appraised at a value of less than ninety thousand dollars and, of course, your horses, which to be honest, Mr. Jackson, are only worth as much to the bank as the current price offered by glue factories.''

The man's face flushed as he slowly rose to his feet. "Thank you for your time, miss, but my horses are worth a hell of a lot more than glue nags, and I'll never see 'em sold as such."

He reached across her desk to pick up his papers, but Roxey stilled his hand with a touch from hers. There were two things Roxey understood and appreciated about Russell Jackson: one was his strong belief in his own abilities and the other was his pride. The first she'd failed to acknowledge. The second she'd damaged severely.

"I'm sorry, Mr. Jackson. I didn't mean to offend you. I was only explaining to you the bank's position." She smiled slightly in an attempt to take the sting out of her words. "We aren't in the horse business. We're in the money business. What loans we make, we want to make darn sure are profitable."

She relaxed against the back of her chair as she gestured to the chair he'd vacated. "Sit down, Mr. Jackson. Let's look over your figures again. Perhaps there are some adjustments we can make that will make your loan application more appealing when I present it to our board."

Roxey spent more than two hours with Russell Jackson, going over and over his prospectus, searching out potential problems, cutting and thinning until the prospectus nearly squeaked it was so tight. As he explained his plans to her, she found herself caught up in his enthusiasm for his horse farm. Without trying, he'd won her respect as well as her confidence.

When they finished, they shook hands, and Russell left, leaving behind his prospectus. But he didn't leave the bank empty-handed—he took with him Roxanne Classen's promise to do her best to obtain the loan for him.

After Russell left, Roxey glanced at her calendar. The loan board met the first and third Wednesdays of each month. They were due to meet again in two days. When they did, she would be there with Russell Jackson's prospectus in her hands. It was the first loan proposal she would carry to the board. That, coupled with the fact that she believed in Russell's idea, made her determined to win approval for him.

On the morning of the board meeting when Roxey took her seat in the only remaining chair at the table, cigar smoke already permeated the air of the conference room. From his position at the head of the table, J.P. Classen—chairman of the board and the bank's majority stockholder—glanced up and frowned at his daughter's late entrance.

"Now that everyone's here, we can get started. Let's begin with the real estate loans. Thomas, you lead off."

With that, J.P. Classen reared back in his chair, templed his fingers together and listened as Thomas Hightower presented each loan application and made recommendations on each. Roxey sat on the edge of her chair and listened intently to each case. Today was the first time she had sat in on a meeting, and she intended to learn all she could.

Then it was her turn. Her father glanced at her. "Roxey, I understand you have a business loan for our consideration. Let's hear what you've got."

As she stood, Roxey handed a stack of papers to the man on her left. "I'm passing around a copy of the prospectus under consideration. Section A contains sketches of the projected buildings and corrals. Section B contains the applicant's financial statement. Section C is a projected profit-and-loss statement for the horse farm. Section D gives a list of the property Mr. Jackson is putting up for collateral. Section E describes in detail the nature of the business, including a list of all competitors within a ten-state span."

Roxey heard a chuckle from the man on her left but ignored it. "I've spent a great deal of time with Mr. Jackson, walking over his land, inspecting the property, and it's my opinion that the bank should make the loan. If you have any questions, I'll be glad to answer them."

Roxey waited. There was another chuckle. She watched the man sitting across from her flip through the prospectus, giving each page only a cursory glance. Another board member—Charles Glidden, a senior loan officer—didn't even bother to pick up his copy of the prospectus from the table. He gave Roxey a patronizing smile.

Realization hit as she glanced around the table. Men. All men. And the one closest to her own age was probably Frank Turner, who had turned forty last week. She knew because she'd seen the bouquet of black balloons the secretaries in his department had sent him. It was then she realized the futility of her proposal. To them she was a kid, who had a lot to learn about the banking business.

J.P. cleared his throat. "I think we all agree that there isn't enough collateral to cover the size of the loan requested. Application denied. Are there any other—"

"Wait just a minute." Roxey took a deep breath to calm her shaking voice. "Granted the ratio between the collateral and the requested loan amount is marginal, but the opportunity for large profits in the future is here."

Charles Glidden snorted. "This isn't Las Vegas, Roxanne. We're bankers, not gamblers."

A burst of laughter followed his sarcastic remark. In desperation, she looked to her father. Obviously, he had requested no special consideration be given his daughter—and the officers were doing a wonderful job of carrying out his request.

With a jerk of his head, J.P. Classen gestured for her to sit down. Anger rose, warming her face as she reluctantly took her seat. She might have lost this round, but she definitely wasn't giving up the fight. She would do more research and be back at the next board meeting with both guns loaded.

When she returned to her office, Roxey found her mail on her desk. Still feeling the bite of the board's rejection of her loan recommendation, she listlessly flipped through the stack. A Department of Public Education, State of Kentucky, return address caught her attention, and she snatched up the letter and ripped it open. When she unfolded the letterhead, a newspaper clipping fell onto her desk. She picked it up and read:

Help Wanted: Mature adult to drive two children to after-school activities. Salary open. Respond to Seth Dandridge, Rte. 3, Box 85, Shelbyville, KY.

She quickly picked up the letter and scanned LaVerne Higgenbotham's carefully penned handwriting. After reading it a second time, more slowly, she slumped back in her chair, tears building in her eyes.

LaVerne's letter came too soon on the heels of her defeat with the loan board. She missed LaVerne and would have given anything to be able to sit down with her right now over a glass of lime tea and tell her about her disappointments with the bank.

Roxey spun her chair around and stared through a blur of tears out her window at the Louisville skyline. This was what she'd wanted. This was what she'd worked twelve months with the state in order to obtain, so why wasn't she happy? It wasn't just the fact that the board hadn't approved her first loan. No, it went beyond that.

Then what was it? She glanced down at the newspaper clipping she still held in her fingertips. Seth Dandridge. He was the root of her unhappiness. She missed him and his children.

She read the classified ad again. So he hadn't found anyone to drive the children yet. A smile began to spread across her face. She wheeled her chair around and started yanking open drawers and throwing in papers in a wild attempt to clean off her desk.

After grabbing her purse and jacket, she flew out of her office, calling to her secretary as she hurried by, ''I'm gone for the day. If anyone asks, I'm out looking at potential investments. See you in the morning.''

Forty-five minutes later, when Roxey climbed out of her car at the Dandridge farm, there wasn't a soul in sight. Now that she was there, doubts plagued her. Seth hadn't contacted her since he'd left her town house weeks ago. What if he didn't want to see her? What if— She blocked out the negative thoughts. She was here. There was no turning back now.

She walked around the side of the house just as Seth stepped from the barn. He dropped the latch board across the door to bolt it, then turned and headed in the direction of the house. Halfway there, he glanced up. When he saw Roxey, he stopped in midstride, staring at her for a moment as if he didn't trust his eyes. She lifted her hand and waved. For a moment, she feared he would turn and walk the other way. But then he walked on toward her, his steps heavier, a little slower than before.

"Hi, Seth."

"Hello, Roxey."

Nervously, she glanced around. "Where are the children?"

"At Miss Bertha's. I dropped them off at lunchtime. She's teaching Cissy to embroider while Brandon takes care of some chores for her."

"Oh. I see." Roxey clasped her hands behind her back, unable to take her eyes off him. He'd let his hair grow long again, and he was wearing faded jeans and a sweat-stained shirt under a down vest. Yes, and darn it, he looked good, more handsome than she'd ever seen him look.

"I don't want to keep you from your work. I just dropped in to say hello."

"It's okay. I'm finished at the barn. I was on my way up to the house to clean up. Would you like a cup of coffee?"

"How long has it been brewing?"

Seth smiled sheepishly. "About two hours."

"Yuck! Thick and bitter. I think I'll pass."

He laughed, breaking the strained atmosphere that stretched between them. "I guess you could start a fresh pot while I wash up."

When Seth stepped from the bathroom just off the kitchen, he had a hand towel wrapped around his neck. His hair and beard were damp from the water he'd splashed on his face. His cheeks—the part not covered by his beard—glowed a healthy rose from the scrubbing.

He walked into the kitchen, pulled a chair out from the table and twirled it around on one leg to straddle it. Roxey brought two cups of coffee to the table, placing one in front of Seth.

After a slow deliberate sip, he looked at her. "Heard you quit your job."

"Yes, my year was up. I'm a loan officer at the bank in Louisville."

He stared in silent anger at his coffee cup. All his fears of Roxey needing the city life were jelling right before his eyes. "Guess you finally got what you wanted."

Roxey caught her lower lip between her teeth before answering. "Maybe."

He lifted his gaze from his cup to Roxey's face. "Is all not well in paradise?"

"Yes and no." She sighed deeply. "The board denied my first loan application today."

If he could have saved her from the realities of life, he would have, but knowing firsthand how cruel the business world could be made him reply, "You win some, you lose some."

She frowned at what she considered to be his condescending tone. "It's not myself I'm concerned about." She stood and walked to the sink, nursing the cup's warmth between her hands. "The loan was for a young man just starting out. He wants to raise registered quarter horses. He already has a start, but needs the additional capital to expand into a profit-making business. Unfortunately, he doesn't have much collateral."

"Welcome to the real world."

Roxey wheeled around, her eyes flashing. "Why do you have to be so...so...cynical? The *real world*, as you call it, isn't always bad. And besides, how would you know what the real world is like when you hide yourself away here on the farm?"

His eyes darkened perceptibly and immediately she regretted her words.

"I'm sorry. I didn't mean that. It's just that the board's decision really hurt."

"I suppose you're going to quit. Give up. The spoiled little girl didn't get her way so she's going to take her toys and go home."

Roxey sucked in an angry breath. "I am *not* quitting. I'm going to do more research and present my case to the board again. And *again*, if necessary, until they agree to loan Russell the money."

"If that's the case, then what are you doing here in the middle of the afternoon?"

His question caught Roxey by surprise. She searched her mind for an explanation. "Well, because...I...uh...I received a letter from my supervisor at the state today, and she enclosed a clipping of your ad." Regaining some of her composure, she added, "It looks as if you haven't upheld your end of our bargain."

Seth slammed his cup down, splashing coffee on the oilcloth table covering. "So that's it. You're checking up on us. I should've known this wasn't a social visit." He glared at her a moment before adding, "Not that it's your business anymore, but no, I haven't found anyone."

Roxey puffed up, her voice rising in righteous indignation. "It is, too, my business. You made a deal with me, Seth Dandridge. In exchange for my approval on your application, you agreed to involve the children in outside activities. And my quitting my job doesn't nullify that agreement."

Seth glared back at her. "It isn't as if I haven't tried. There just doesn't seem to be anyone interested in the job. And just because I haven't found someone to drive them doesn't mean they aren't going."

She hadn't come here to argue, she had come because she missed him. So why was she spending precious time arguing with him? Roxey returned to the table and sat down opposite him. He turned his face away, refusing to meet her gaze, obviously still angry with her. But in that split second of eyeing each other face-to-face, she noticed something she'd missed earlier. Dark circles lay beneath his eyes, and his cheekbones seemed more pronounced.

Without having to ask, Roxey knew why. Seth was driving the children himself. Taking time from an already overloaded schedule to see that he upheld his end of the bargain.

The ticking of the kitchen clock grew loud in the silence, reminding her again of the time. Her hands clasped tightly around the mug, Roxey suddenly blurted out, "I'll do it."

Seth's face wrinkled in confusion. "You'll do what?"

"I'll drive the children to their activities."

Seth held up a hand to stop her. "Now wait a minute. You already have a job."

"I'm aware of that. But the children's activities shouldn't begin until after five o'clock, and I can easily leave work at four. So there shouldn't be a problem."

"Think about what you're saying! You'd be driving back and forth every day from Louisville. It just doesn't make sense."

He argued on, but Roxey turned a deaf ear to him. Finally, when it appeared he'd run out of arguments, Roxey took a pen and paper from her purse and smiled at Seth. "What are the children's schedules?"

Seconds ticked by while Seth sat in frustrated silence. Finally, he shook his head in defeat as he began to go over the children's schedules. "Brandon has soccer practice on Monday, Wednesday and Friday at five-thirty, and games on Thursdays at six and Saturdays at nine in the morning. Cissy has ballet on Tuesday at five-fifteen and Brownies on Thursday at five-thirty, but I'm not going to let you—"

She smiled at him, completely disarming him with her unconcern. "I'll be here Monday by five. Tell the children to be ready. Cissy and I can do the grocery shopping while Brandon's at practice, so why don't you have a list made for us?"

Grudgingly, Seth said, "All right, but I won't allow you to drive back to Louisville alone at night. It just wouldn't be safe. You can stay here with us and commute. But this is only until I find someone to take the job. Agreed?"

"Agreed." Hoping to escape before he changed his mind, Roxey glanced at her watch. "Gee, look at the time. I've got to run. I told LaVerne I'd come by the office and see her before five." She stood and hurried to the door. "Tell the children I said hello and I'll see them Monday."

And she was gone. He watched the curtains sway from the impact of the door's slam until they grew still. Good Lord! Had he really asked her to live with them?

LaVerne wrapped her thin arms around Roxey and hugged her tight, then stepped back and held her at arm's length. "My, how I've missed you." She hugged her again, then released her. "Come in and sit down. Tell me what you're doing in Shelbyville."

Roxey walked into what had formerly been her office and glanced around the room with a pang of longing. "I've been out to the Dandridges'."

LaVerne lifted one eyebrow. "You have, huh? And what were you doing at the Dandridges'?"

"Applying for a job."

LaVerne's jaw sagged open. "What happened to your job at the bank?"

"Nothing. I still have it."

"Well, for heaven's sake. When I sent you that clipping, I certainly didn't intend for *you* to apply for the job! I only wanted you to know Mr. Dandridge was trying to uphold his end of the bargain."

"I know that, LaVerne." Roxey ducked her head and studied the nail polish on her thumbnail. "Your letter made me homesick, so I decided to take the afternoon off and come for a visit."

"Homesick?" LaVerne cocked her head to study Roxey. "Folks who're homesick are usually pining away for their home and family." She leaned closer and put a finger under Roxey's chin, and lifted until Roxey's gaze met hers. "Is there something you need to tell me, Roxey?"

Eleven

All the fears Roxey had voiced to LaVerne of Seth's changing his mind and turning her away were for naught. When she arrived at the farm on Monday afternoon, Brandon and Cissy were sitting on the front steps. Brandon, wearing a sweat suit and tennis shoes, was tossing a soccer ball back and forth between his hands while Cissy chattered away at his side. Seth was nowhere in sight.

When Cissy spotted Roxey, she jumped up from the porch steps and ran toward the car, waving a piece of paper in her hand.

By the time Roxey parked and opened the car door, Cissy was breathless. "You and me are going to the grocery store after we take Brandon to practice. Daddy gave me the list and—" she stopped long enough to pat the pocket of her blue jeans "—he gave me the grocery money. It's right here and I'm not s'posed to take it out till we get to the store."

Roxey laughed gaily as she knelt and gave Cissy a quick hug. "Well, aren't you something?" She turned to Brandon. "Hi, Brandon. Are you ready for practice?"

His gaze on the ball, Brandon continued to toss it, refusing to look at Roxey. "Yeah, I guess."

He walked to the car, climbed in the back and slumped against the seat without another word. Roxey blew out a long breath. Well, one thing hadn't changed.

After dropping Brandon at the practice field, Roxey drove on to the shopping center. "What have you been doing since I saw you last, Cissy?"

Cissy screwed up her face as she tried to remember. "Well, we came back home and unpacked our suitcases, then Daddy made us carry our dirty clothes to the laundry room, then—"

Roxey laughed. "No, Cissy. I don't mean *everything* you've done. Just general things. Like, are you having school at home? Things like that."

"Oh." Cissy sighed with relief. "Well, let's see. Daddy's been teaching me to read. But I don't think I'm doing very good." Tears welled in her eyes. "He fusses at me sometimes. And he hardly ever smiles anymore."

Roxey reached over, caught Cissy's hand in hers and squeezed. "Oh, I bet it's not you. He probably just has a lot on his mind with the farm and all. And besides, now that I'm here, I can help you with your lessons, too. What do you think about that?"

A smile lit Cissy's face. "Would you really, Miss Classen?"

"Yes, really. In fact we'll start tonight."

Roxey and the Dandridges fell into an easy routine. The children were always ready and waiting when Roxey arrived home from work. Then, while she was out running them around to their different activities, Seth did the evening chores and started dinner. After dinner, Roxey cleaned up the kitchen while Seth and the children settled down at the table for an hour or two of studying. When time allowed, Roxey joined them at the table to help Cissy.

It was an even distribution of responsibility. Roxey found a comfortableness in their routine, a sense of family that she silently welcomed, although she soon discovered Cissy was right in saying Seth didn't smile much anymore. He was polite to Roxey and attentive to the children, but there seemed to be a discontent seeded deep within him. At the first opportunity, Roxey intended to find out what was bothering him.

Unfortunately, the occasion never seemed to arise. When he wasn't helping with the children, Seth barricaded himself in the barn. One of the cows was going to calve any day and had already shown signs of a difficult delivery. Determined to save both the cow and the calf, Seth spent every spare minute in the barn, working on equipment while keeping a watchful eye on the expectant cow.

Friday night, after Roxey had been at the farm nearly a week, Seth slipped into her room in the middle of the night and touched a hand to her shoulder. Gently shaking her, he whispered, "Roxey. Wake up."

"What's wrong?" she asked as she rolled to her back, rubbing her eyes sleepily.

"Ssshh," he warned. "Nothing's wrong. I want you to come out to the barn."

Roxey glanced at the darkened window. "Now?"

He chuckled softly. "Yes, now. Put on some clothes and meet me there. I've got a surprise for you."

Grudgingly, Roxey rose and pulled on a thick sweatshirt and jeans.

Shivering against the cold, she ran to the barn, mumbling curses on Seth for waking her in the middle of the night. When she pulled the barn door closed behind her, Seth turned from the stall door he'd been peering over.

He was smiling.

Roxey wasn't.

"This better be good," she threatened, her eyes narrowed in warning.

Chuckling good-naturedly, Seth motioned for Roxey to join him at the stall door. His height allowed him to peer over the top of the door, but Roxey was forced to peek through its slats.

All signs of her ill humor quickly vanished.

"Twins!" she squealed as she clambered up two slats of the door to get a better look at the two white-faced calves nursing at the mother cow's udder. "Oh, Seth. Aren't they adorable?"

Seth caught Roxey around the waist to steady her. "I don't know if I'd choose that particular word to describe them, but yes, they *are* kind of cute."

The cow swung her head around and mooed, rolling wild eyes at the humans intruding on her privacy.

"I think the old bossy is getting a little riled. Maybe we better leave them alone for a while."

Reluctantly, Roxey lowered her foot to catch the slat below her, but missed. While beating the empty air in search of a foothold, she lost her grip on the door and slid down the rough wood.

Immediately, Seth was at her side. "Are you hurt?"

Roxey squeezed her right hand in her left. "No, but I think I got a splinter."

"Let me see."

She held out her hand for his inspection. A splinter of wood pierced her palm, the skin around it already turning an angry red. "Come with me." Seth led her to the storeroom.

Once inside, he picked Roxey up and plunked her down on a saddle that was draped over a wooden workhorse. After fetching the first-aid kit, Seth dug out a pair of tweezers and a tube of antiseptic ointment.

"Hold out your hand."

Biting at her lip, Roxey watched as Seth probed at the splinter. "Ouch!"

He glanced up. "Sorry. Hang on. I've almost got it." With a quick jerk of his hand, he removed the splinter and held it up for Roxey's inspection. "Big enough for a toothpick. Want to keep it for a souvenir?"

Wrinkling her nose at him, Roxey replied dryly, "No thanks. You can have it."

Seth picked up the tube of antiseptic and squirted some onto his finger. Gingerly, he took Roxey's hand and began to smear the ointment over her palm. At his soft touch, tingles ricocheted from her hand throughout her body, igniting answering responses in every nerve.

Seth knew he had rubbed on enough cream to heal twenty wounds, but he couldn't bring himself to release her hand. The pleasure of simply holding it was almost more than he could bear. His pulse pounded in his ears, and his fingers trembled as they smoothed across her palm.

Roxey swallowed hard, then lifted her eyes from their joined hands to find Seth's heated gaze focused on her. The gentle rubbing of his fingers slowed. His gaze still locked on hers, he lifted her hand and placed her fingertips at his lips.

"Does it feel better now?" he whispered.

The movement of his lips, soft as velvet and warm as a summer breeze, caressed her fingers. Breathless, Roxey could only nod.

For weeks, she had willed herself to forget the gentleness of his touch, to blot out the knee-weakening memory of his passion. But with him standing so close, the heat of his body emanating warm against hers, it all rushed back to her, blinding her to all but the excruciating desire to be in his arms.

Seth saw the desire flame in her eyes and felt an answering one kindle low in his groin. He hadn't planned this. He'd only wanted to share his excitement over the calves with her. But now with her so close, the temptation to hold her was overpowering. "Roxey, I . . ."

Not sure who moved first, Roxey found herself swallowed up in his embrace, her cheek pressed flat against the wall of his chest. The pounding of his heart thundered at her ear, matching the pace of her own quickened pulse.

She tipped her head back and looked deep into his dark brown eyes. Hot, piercing, knowing, his gaze moved over her, fanning the fire within her that only he could put out. Filling his hands with her wild mane of hair, he lowered his face to meet hers. Their lips touched, then fused in response to the red-hot passion that flamed within.

Hungry for the feel of her body pressed against his, Seth smoothed his hands down her back, cupping her buttocks in the span of his broad hands, fitting himself in the narrow V between her legs. The action only served to frustrate him. He wanted all of her. To feel the satiny softness of her bare skin beneath his. To fill her with the passion that raged within him.

He pulled her hands from around his neck and stepped from her embrace, clasping her hands tightly in his. "Come with me."

It wasn't a question, requiring an answer. Nor a command she was expected to obey. It was a tacit understanding between the two. Silently, Roxey followed him from the storeroom and up the ladder to the hayloft above.

Hay was stacked high in the loft in preparation for the long winter months ahead. Though the days were still warm, the nights were cool and Roxey shivered, rubbing her hands up and down her arms as she watched Seth pull a tarp from a pile in the corner.

After shaking out the canvas cloth, Seth spread it out over the loose hay on the floor of the loft, shaping a makeshift bed. In the time it had taken to climb to the loft, an awkwardness had grown between them, banking the passions that had flared only moments before. Not knowing how to breach it, Seth stood on one side of the tarp and Roxey on the other.

He lifted a hand, then let it drop. "I wish I could offer you better, but with the kids in the house . . ."

"That's okay." Wanting to reassure him, Roxey added with a smile, "I guess I'm becoming a little bit country. A bed of hay sounds divine."

Seth brushed a few pieces of straw from the tarp, the accompanying cloud of dust making him sneeze.

Roxey said "Bless you," automatically.

Seth glanced up, a half grin on his face. "I think I'm allergic to hay."

Roxey frowned at him. "Allergic to hay? A farmer?"

Moving to stand in front of her, he wrapped his arms loosely at her waist. "Maybe it's the combination of hay and you. Whenever I'm around the two of you at the same time, I get this itch. . . ."

"Oh, you." Roxey pushed at his chest, but he caught her up in his arms, laughing, and lifted her up until their lips met.

"Want to scratch that itch?" he asked.

Roxey felt his teasing smile against her lips. Deciding to play along with his game, she said, "What itch?"

Seth loosened his grip and let her slide slowly down the length of him, enjoying the feel of her body chafing against his. "There's one here." He pointed to his cheek.

Roxey placed her lips there and feathered a kiss.

"And here." He pointed to the hollow of his throat. When her warm lips touched there, he quickly dropped his hand to his chest. "And here."

Pearlized snaps popped open under Roxey's hand as she dragged her finger down the front of Seth's Western-style shirt. When his chest was bared, she pressed her lips against the springy hair, then touched her tongue where his finger had rested only moments before.

Her fevered touch knifed through Seth. Groaning deeply, he quickly shrugged out of his shirt and scooped Roxey up into his arms. At the edge of the tarp, he knelt and gently placed Roxey on the bed of sweet-smelling hay. His eyes burned with intensity as he gazed at her uplifted face. "I want you, Roxey. God, how I want you."

"And I want you."

In the moonlight filtering through the barn's dust-covered window, Roxey saw the uncertainty in Seth's face. Knowing the cause for his hesitation, she smoothed her hand across the deep furrows creasing his brow. "It's okay. I'm protected now."

Relief quickly gave way to passion as Seth pulled Roxey into the fold of his arms. She melted against him, the loneliness and uncertainty of the past forgotten in his embrace. While his lips challenged her to meet his raging hunger, his fingers roamed over her, the goose bumps he drew a contradiction to the fever burning beneath her skin.

She met his challenge and issued one of her own. A sense of urgency overtook their lovemaking, each desperate to make up for the weeks they'd been apart. Shoes, socks, jeans and shirts were discarded one by one, until nothing but air separated Roxey from Seth. That, too, disappeared when Seth lowered himself over her and buried himself deep within her, whispering her name over and over again as he filled her with the pulsing heat of his desire.

The next morning Seth woke to the sound of the rooster crowing. He glanced at the clock beside the bed. Six o'clock. Damn! He'd overslept. It had been after three when he and Roxey had returned to the house, and his head throbbed from the effects of too little sleep.

Daylight brought with it a reality the darkness in the barn had helped conceal. He pressed a weary hand across his eyes and closed them against the memory of the night with Roxey. It had been a mistake. A big mistake. He never should have made love with her again. Doubling up his fist, he slammed it against the mattress as he pushed himself off the bed. He couldn't allow himself to get involved with her. She didn't belong on his farm and never would.

After jerking a pair of clean jeans from his chest of drawers, he crossed to the bathroom and twisted on the shower. Cold water shot from the shower head, pelting him with its icy spray. It had the desired sobering effect. He had to stay away from Roxey. Keep a safe distance. That was the only way he could keep himself from making love with her again.

He twisted the faucet to a warmer temperature and began to lather up. Someone to drive the children to their activities was what he needed. Once he solved that problem, there would be no reason for Roxey to hang around.

The realization made him sag back against the tiled shower wall, his arms limp at his sides. He remembered the last time he'd watched her drive away and the subsequent pain that had twisted in his gut. Would he be able to let her leave again?

Lying in her bed in the Dandridges' guest room, Roxey smiled and stretched like a cream-filled cat as she reflected on the stolen hours she'd spent in Seth's arms. Though she would have gladly spent the night in the barn with him, Seth had insisted they return to the house and the comfort of their own beds. She brushed her hand across the cotton sheet beside her, knowing full well a bed of hay—if shared with Seth—would have suited her more.

She glanced at the clock and sighed deeply. Seth was probably gone by now and it was time to wake up the children. Any other Saturday morning she would have slept in, but last night she had promised Seth she would take Brandon to his soccer game while Seth drove into Louisville to pick up a piece of equipment he'd ordered.

With so many responsibilities to take care of, the morning flew by for Roxey, and when the soccer game was over, she stopped by Miss Bertha's house to drop off the children. She turned down the invitation to stay and make taffy on the pretext she had a week's worth of laundry to catch up on. The laundry did in fact overflow the hamper, but her true reason for returning home was the hope of catching Seth alone.

With two loads of wet sheets piled into a laundry basket, Roxey headed for the backyard and the clothesline. She clipped the wooden clothespins in place. She laughed out loud at the thought of her friend Justine's face if she saw her now.

Roxey's housekeeping skills had always been minimal. When she and Justine were roommates in college, Roxey's half of their room had always been a mess. Only when Justine threatened to hire a maid and charge the fee to Roxey's parents would Roxey finally give in and clean it up. Back in July when Roxey had called Justine and canceled out on the trip to the Bahamas, her friend had accepted Roxey's reason without batting an eye. She of all people was accustomed to Roxey's impetuousness and in subsequent conversations referred to Roxey's week on the Dandridges' farm as her "wilderness adventure."

Seth stepped from the barn, wiping his hands on a handkerchief. He stopped when he saw the sheets flapping on the line and watched for a moment as Roxey moved about, bending to pick up a sheet, then stretching her arms upward to pin it to the thin clothesline wire. He started toward her, then stopped, frowning as he remembered his vow to keep a safe distance.

But he couldn't ignore her, he reasoned. After all, they were sharing the same house. And it was broad daylight. What could happen outside in broad daylight in front of God and everybody? Roxey's soft laughter drifted across the yard to Seth, and he couldn't help smiling himself as he walked toward her, confident he could keep his vow.

"I never found anything funny about hanging out sheets to dry. Want to share your secret?"

Roxey wheeled around, the smile disappearing as she squinted up at Seth. "Gracious! You startled me."

She stood on her toes and pecked his cheek, taking Seth by surprise. Then she smiled again. To Seth, her smile was like throwing sunshine on a cloudy day.

"I was just thinking about something a friend of mine said." She stooped to move the basket, but Seth took it from her.

"Here. I'll do that. It's too heavy for you."

Roxey fought back a smile. Too heavy, huh? She wondered how he thought that heavy basket made it from the house to the backyard.

"Thanks." She pulled a sheet from the pile, draped two corners over the line and slipped a clothespin in place. "The children are down at Miss Bertha's making taffy."

Seth picked up a clothespin and stretched the sheet down the line, pinning the opposite end.

The sharp smell of bleach filled the air as the breeze caught the sheets and whipped them around Seth and Roxey as they worked.

"There's nothing better than sleeping on sweet-smelling, line-dried sheets." Roxey's voice sounded dreamy as she voiced her thoughts, then with a sigh she dipped her hand back into the basket. "But we won't be able to hang them out much longer. Before long it'll be too cold."

Seth glanced at her. Sometimes she surprised him with her comments. He'd have thought she would prefer her satin sheets to his line-dried, cotton ones. He watched her shake out another sheet, catching it neatly by the corners before clipping it to the line.

Her movements drew his gaze to her faded University of Kentucky sweatshirt. About four sizes too big for her, the shirt hung almost to Roxey's knees. The basket of wet sheets at his feet was forgotten as he watched the fleece fabric rise to cup her jean-clad buttocks as Roxey stretched to clip the pin to the line.

When Seth didn't pick up the other end of the sheet, Roxey turned to him and caught him staring at her. Flustered, he grabbed the corners she held out to him and quickly pinned the sheet into place.

The basket now empty, he stepped back and stuffed his hands deep into his pockets. "Well, I guess I better get back to work."

"Do you want some lunch? Miss Bertha sent a pot of stew."

Seth squinted one eye up at the sun. "Yeah, I guess it's about lunchtime." A man has to eat, he reasoned to himself. He picked up the empty basket and walked with her to the house.

While he washed up, Roxey put steaming bowls of homemade stew on the table. She had just poured the iced tea when Seth took his seat at the table. When she leaned across him to place his drink beside his bowl, she rested a hand in the middle of his back. It was a simple gesture, one that probably meant nothing, but he felt the warmth of her hand long after she'd removed it and had seated herself across from him.

Seth forced a smile as he dipped his spoon into his bowl, and filled it with chunks of vegetables. "Looks good."

Still basking in the afterglow of their night of lovemaking, Roxey leaned back in her chair, content just to look at him. Seeing his smile reminded her of Cissy's comment about the lack of it. "It's good to see you smile, Seth. We've missed it."

He paused, looking up at Roxey over the spoonful of steaming stew. "I didn't realize I hadn't been."

She shrugged as she stirred her spoon around and around her soup bowl. "Cissy mentioned to me that you never smiled anymore. And, well—" she glanced up to meet his gaze "—you *have* seemed different. Like you're unhappy. Is something bothering you?"

Slowly he lowered his spoon to his bowl, then rested his wrists against the edge of the tabletop. "No. Nothing's wrong." Suddenly, he pushed away from the table. "I better get back to work." He grabbed his jacket from the coat hook by the back door and called as he went out, "Thanks for the lunch."

Seth returned to the barn and his work there, escaping Roxey's probing look and questions, but not the frustration her questions had spurred. Had he been so obvious that even his six-year-old daughter could read his mood? Seth leaned his weight against the wrench, struggling to loosen a bolt on the baler he was working on. He didn't want anyone to know how much it hurt to have Roxey around . . . or how much worse it had been when she wasn't. Frustrated with the frozen bolt and even more with his feelings for Roxey, Seth threw the wrench against the barn wall where it hit with a loud thud.

Raking his fingers through his hair, he sagged back against the baler as the wrench clattered against the concrete floor. God! Why had he allowed her back in their lives? Last night was proof enough he couldn't trust himself alone with her. Was he so stupid he had to have it shoved in his face twice before he was willing to admit she was out of his league? No, dammit! Seth Dandridge had made one mistake by lowering the barriers he'd erected around his heart. He didn't intend to make another one.

"Seth?"

He heard her calling him as she made her way through the barn. Quickly, he retrieved the wrench from the floor and began to tug on the bolt again. "Over here."

She rounded the bulky machine and stopped at his side. "Can we talk?"

His breath was labored as he tugged on the bolt, his biceps bulging beneath the sleeves of his shirt as he put all his strength behind the wrench. "Not now. I'm busy."

"When then?"

He released his grip long enough to wipe the sweat from his forehead in the crook of his arm. His voice was sharp with impatience as he leaned into the wrench again. "I don't know. Just later, okay?"

Roxey stepped around him until she faced him. Her voice shook with tightly controlled emotion. "No. I think we need to talk now."

Without looking up, he said, "Fine. Then talk."

"I love you, Seth."

The bolt gave, and the sudden release of tension made Seth fall against the machine. He took his time pushing away and straightening up. Pulling a grease-stained rag from his back pocket, he slowly wiped his hands.

Tears built in Roxey's eyes. "Why are you so afraid of admitting you love me, too?"

Seth stuffed the rag in his back pocket and stooped to pick up the wrench where it had fallen on the floor beneath the machine. He tossed it into the toolbox on the floor, then turned to Roxey, his hands pushing at the waist of his jeans. "I'm not afraid."

"Then why do you insist on being so stubborn?"

With a derisive snort, he turned away and picked up a grease gun. "How long have you got?"

Roxey stood her ground. "Long enough."

He squatted down and placed the nozzle of the gun in the hole where the bolt had been and slowly squeezed the trigger. "I'm too old. You're too young. I'm a dirt farmer. You're a blue-blooded snob." He paused, scooted on the balls of his feet until he was even with the next hole and inserted the nozzle. "I've got two kids to raise, Roxey. I don't need a third."

He stood and tossed the gun onto the worktable behind him.

"You don't fool me, Seth Dandridge." Her reply was threaded with a thick layer of steel. She stepped closer until only a foot of space separated them. "Yes, you're older than me, but personally I don't see that as a problem. And as for being a snob, I think you've got that backward. *You're* the snob. I've never once asked you to change anything about yourself. I've accepted you just as you are. But it seems that you can't accept me."

Her voice softened as she raised her hand to his cheek. "And I'm not a child. I thought I'd proved that to you last night."

Her touch tore through all his carefully built barriers. With a muffled oath, he crushed her to him, burying his face in her hair. He kissed her hair, her forehead, scattering kisses across her face as he whispered in a husky voice, "Yes, you've proved that." His lips found hers, and his arms tightened around her, squeezing her like a vise. "Oh, Roxey, Roxey. Don't you see? It'll never work." He caught her face between his hands, forcing her head back in order to meet her gaze. "We come from two different worlds."

His hands tightened on her cheeks. "I can never give you the things you're accustomed to. The farm's all I have. All I want. You'd never be happy here."

"But, I—"

He pressed his thumbs against her lips, silencing her. "No, Roxey. Don't. You don't know what you're saying. You're young yet. How long would it take before you tired of the farm? A month? Six months? Right now it's fun for you. Something different. But eventually the newness would wear off, and it'd lose its appeal for you."

He took a deep breath, his eyes pleading for her understanding. "Be my friend, Rox. But don't ask for more. I don't have it to give."

Raw emotion burned the back of Roxey's throat, threatening to choke her. Seth *did* have it to give. He'd already given her more love than she'd ever known in her life. She wanted more than his friendship, but as she looked into his pain-filled eyes, she knew she would have to accept what he offered—at least for now.

With her eyes squeezed shut against the tears, she turned her lips into his palm, tasting the grease and sweat, feeling the roughness of his callused hands.

She lifted her gaze to his as she promised in a soft whisper, "I'll always be your friend, Seth."

Twelve

Roxey worked hard at being Seth's friend and even harder to hide her love from him. Sometimes as they worked together, her feelings would swell so tightly in her chest she was sure she would suffocate. For Seth's part, he accepted her friendship and in return gave her his, although he was always careful to keep a safe distance between them.

With such a busy schedule to maintain, they all worked together, trying to accomplish as many tasks as possible in one setting. These were the times Roxey loved best.

On one of those unseasonably warm autumn days, just before winter claims the air with its chilly fingers, Seth, Roxey and the children worked in the garden, preparing it for the possibility of an early frost.

"Cissy, what letter does carrot begin with?"

Cissy lifted her head, a puzzled look wrinkling her pert nose. "Kuh, kuh, karrots. Karrots starts with a *k*."

"No. But that's a good guess. There are two letters that make the 'kuh' sound. One is the letter *k* and the other is ... ?"

"C."

"Good, Cissy!"

Seth crawled farther down the vegetable row on his hands and knees, bunching up mulch to protect the plants from the cold. "Brandon, what vitamins are found in carrots?"

"Ah, Dad. Do we have to do this?"

"Yes, we have to do this. Just pretend you're sitting in science or maybe health class, but instead of a stuffy old schoolroom, you're getting to meet outside. Now, what vitamins are found in carrots?"

Brandon scratched the hand rake carefully around the mounds of spinach as he grudgingly began to list, "Vitamin C, vitamin A..."

His voice droned on as he named first the vitamins, then the benefits of each for the body's health.

"Daddy?" Cissy stopped digging potatoes and sat back on her heels.

"Yes, Cissy."

"How'd you get so smart?"

Roxey began to dig furiously, trying hard not to laugh.

"I'm not so smart, Cissy."

"Yes, you are. You ask me and Brandon all these questions and you never even look at a book to see if the answer is right. You just know. How can you do that?"

"I'm just older than you both and have had more experience."

"Is Roxey as smart as you?"

Brandon snorted, and Seth shot him a frown, silencing him, before answering Cissy. "Yes, she's as smart as me."

"But she's not as old as you. How come she can be as smart?"

Roxey sank back on her heels and looked at Seth with an impish smile. "Yeah. How come?"

After shooting Roxey a scowl, Seth stopped his work and sat down on the ground, resting his wrists on his knees. "There are different kinds of smart. Some people have book smarts. Others have a common-sense kind of smarts. When you go to school and study, you get the book kind. You get the common-sense kind by living and learning. That's what

I mean when I say learn by experience. Then there's the kind of smart Roxey is—a smart aleck. Now that—''

A dirt clod on the shoulder silenced him. "Hey!" Seth scooped up a handful of the moist dirt from the freshly hoed garden row and threw it, hitting Roxey on the back of the head when she ducked.

War ensued. Dirt flew back and forth through the air, between the two of them as they alternately fired and ducked, laughing gaily. Roxey quickly realized Seth had the advantage. His hands were bigger, his aim was sharper and, even as big as he was, he dodged well.

Inspiration came to her when she tripped over the garden hose while beating a hasty retreat.

She grabbed the end of the hose, darted for the faucet and twisted it on.

Seth, busy scraping up more dirt, didn't notice.

"Oh, Se-e-eth," Roxey called in a sweet singsong voice.

He glanced up just as she raised the hose. She fixed her thumb over the end of the nozzle and shot a spray of water over him.

Like an angry bear, he lumbered to his feet, roaring. He shook his head, shooting droplets of water from his hair and beard. His head bent and his body stiff with revenge, he stalked Roxey. She darted to the left, then feinted to the right, all the while with a constant spray of water aimed at Seth. Then suddenly she ran out of hose. Seth bore down on her, and she sprayed for all she was worth, soaking his hair and shirt. Without knowing exactly how it happened, Roxey suddenly realized the hose was in his hands.

"Seth, please." She covered her mouth with her hand as she backed away, giggling nervously. "It was just a game. Come on, Seth. Be a good sport. You know how I hate to get my hair wet."

Without so much as a word, Seth raised the hose. Coward that she was, Roxey darted over to Cissy and pulled the child in front of her.

"You wouldn't hurt your own child, now would you?"

Seth just smiled and turned the hose full blast on the two.

Brandon stood at the side of the garden clapping his hands and whooping encouragement to Seth. "Way to go, Dad! Squirt 'em again!"

Seth smiled and shouted back, "Having a good time, son?"

"Yeah! This is great, Dad."

"Think I should soak 'em some more?"

"Yeah! Go for it, Dad."

Seth turned the hose where Cissy and Roxey cowered together, then suddenly wheeled, shooting a spray of water over Brandon.

"Didn't want you to feel left out, son."

"Seth Dandridge! What in the world is going on?"

Roxey jerked her head around at the sound of the feminine voice. A dark-haired woman stood at the side of the house, her hands on her hips.

"Mama!" Brandon yelled in excitement and took off at a run. Cissy was right behind him, and before anyone had a chance to stop them, both children had wrapped their arms around the woman.

"Brandon! Let go of me." The beautiful woman backed away from the children, her elbows lifted to shoulder height, staring openmouthed at the muddy handprints the children had left on her dress. "Look what you've done! You've ruined my dress."

Roxey watched Brandon's smile dissolve and tears flood Cissy's eyes.

"Clarissa, stop that whimpering this instant! Just look at what you and Brandon have done to my dress. I should be the one crying."

"That's enough, Lorissa. The kids didn't mean to get you dirty. They were just excited." Seth's firm voice cut across the length of the garden as he walked to the faucet and turned the water off.

So, Roxey thought, sizing up the elegantly dressed woman before her, this is the former Mrs. Dandridge. Roxey watched the woman wipe ineffectually at her dress with a handkerchief she'd pulled from her leather purse.

"But just look what they've done," Lorissa continued to complain.

"Brandon. Cissy. Tell your mother you're sorry."

Cissy's voice quivered in a mumbled apology. Brandon looked defiantly at his dad, then turned and ran.

Anger mottled Seth's face as he moved to follow him. Roxey stepped into his path and blocked him. "I'll get him. Maybe you better take Lorissa in the house and let her clean up, then see if you can calm Cissy down."

Seth looked behind Roxey in the direction Brandon had run, then at Cissy. "Okay." He reached out and squeezed Roxey's hand. "Thanks, Rox."

Roxey had learned weeks ago where Brandon's favorite hiding place was: the loft. Filled now with hay, it was the perfect place to hide, offering hundreds of secluded nooks to burrow down in. Fortunately for Roxey, his sniffles gave his hiding place away.

"Brandon?" She knelt down next to him in the hay.

"Go away."

"No. I'm not going away unless you come with me."

"I'm not going back down there."

"But your mother's here to see you."

"I don't want to see her. I hate her."

The raw hurt she heard in his voice squeezed at her heart. "You don't mean that."

He jerked his head around, his dirty face streaked with tears. "How do you know how I feel? I said I hate her and I do."

"No. You're hurt right now and maybe a little angry at your mother, but you don't hate her. Not really."

"Yes, I do!" Great heaving sobs shook his shoulders. "I hate her, and I hate you, too."

"Brandon." Roxey's voice became firm. "You don't mean that."

"Yes, I do. If you weren't always here, Mama would come back and live with us. I know she would."

"I think you know that's not true. Your parents divorced a long time before I ever knew your father."

He turned his head away.

"Didn't they, Brandon?"

Silence.

She pulled him around and gripped him by his arms, knowing she had to make him admit it, if only to himself. "Didn't they, Brandon?"

Roxey watched the anger and hurt build on his face until she feared he would explode with the pent-up emotions.

"Yes!" he finally screamed. "Yes! Yes! Yes!" He dissolved into convulsive sobs.

Roxey pulled him against her breast and held him, letting him cry out his bitterness and his anger, drawing his pain into her own heart. Tears burned her eyes as she shared all the anger and rejection Brandon had experienced at the hand of his selfish mother. When he had calmed, she held him at arm's length, tipping his chin until he was forced to look at her.

"Brandon, how your father and I feel about each other has nothing to do with why your mother and father divorced. You know that, don't you?"

At his reluctant nod, she continued. "No one—not me or anyone else—can ever take your mother's place. She'll always be your mother and nothing can change that. I know you're angry with her right now, but you have to understand that your mother is a little angry with you, too. You didn't mean to mess up her dress, but the fact is you did, didn't you?"

He nodded again as he bit down hard on his lower lip.

"I know you don't really hate your mother. You love her. You wouldn't be so upset right now if you didn't. So why don't you tell me why you're so mad at her?"

Brandon took a deep, shuddery breath. "Because she . . . she doesn't love us."

Roxey felt her heart plummet to her feet. So much pain for a little boy to bear. She lifted her fingers to brush the hair away from his forehead and realized that for all his tough talk, he was still only a boy. "Are you sure she doesn't love you?"

At his silence, Roxey asked, "If she didn't love you, would she come to see you? Or invite you to come and see her? You know what I think? I think you're still mad because she left you and moved away."

Brandon ducked his head, unable to meet Roxey's penetrating gaze, but he couldn't hide from her the tears that spilled, staining the leg of his jeans in small dark circles.

"That was a long time ago, Brandon. Maybe someday you'll understand why she did what she did. But even if you don't you've got to forgive her.

"Sometimes when you don't see someone for long periods of time, you draw a picture in your mind of how that person is. Then when you're with them and they don't act like you thought they should, it disappoints you. Sometimes it may even make you mad. But you have to learn to love your mother for the way she is, not for the way you want her to be. In her way, she loves you."

Seth watched through the kitchen window as Roxey and Brandon emerged from the barn, both dirty and with hay clinging to their damp clothes. He knew Brandon had gone to the hayloft. The boy always did when he was upset about something.

Seth had worried about allowing Roxey to go after his son. Considering the boy's animosity toward her, Seth had been concerned it would only make matters worse. But seeing Roxey walking alongside Brandon with her arm slung across his shoulders, Seth assumed Roxey had been able to smooth things over.

A half smile spread on Brandon's face as Roxey said something to him, and Seth felt a tightening in his chest. Brandon had suffered most from the divorce, probably because he'd been the older child. Old enough to realize his mother was gone, to miss her, to feel the hurt when she rejected him. As a result, Seth had pampered him somewhat, allowing him to get by with things he should have been disciplined for. Being rude to Roxey was one of those things.

As they drew closer to the house, Seth saw where tears had left streaks through the dirt on his son's face. Seth swallowed back a lump of emotion as he turned away from the window.

How was it that life got so twisted?

When the back door opened and Brandon and Roxey stepped into the kitchen, Seth met them. He knelt down and opened his arms to his son, and Brandon fell into them, burying his face in his father's shoulder with a broken sob. Wanting to allow them the privacy they needed to talk, Roxey tiptoed toward the door, but as she passed Seth, he caught her hand in his, stopping her. Looking over his son's tousled hair, he offered her a tremulous smile before squeezing her hand, then letting it go.

Raw emotion tore through Roxey as she made her way to her room. The futility of her position pressed upon her. She was the outsider and always would be. Brandon resented her presence, and God only knew when and if he would ever overcome it. And Seth—a sob caught in Roxey's throat. After seeing his ex-wife, Roxey better understood why Seth didn't trust Roxey's feelings for him or his farm.

As she reached the top of the stairs, Roxey stopped at Cissy's bedroom door. Cissy lay curled up on the bed with her doll, Trixie Gail, clutched tight in her arms. Roxey tiptoed across the room and pulled a light quilt from the foot of the bed to spread over the sleeping child. Of all the Dandridges, Cissy was the only one who loved Roxey without reservation.

After lifting a tendril of hair away from Cissy's face, Roxey feathered a kiss on her cheek. "And I love you, too, Cissy."

Biting back the tears threatening to stream down her face, Roxey crossed to the adjoining bathroom.

A shiver shook her, making her realize her clothes were still damp from the water fight in the garden. Slowly she peeled off the damp clothes and dropped them carelessly to the floor, before stepping into the shower.

Only one drawer remained to be emptied. Roxey picked up the stack of lingerie, walked with it to the bed and stuffed it into her suitcase. She paused to wipe a stray tear from her cheek before zipping the lid and snapping the lock in place.

She heard the wind whining through the trees outside her window and pushed back the curtains to peer out into the darkness. The moon was full, but no stars shone to give relief to the blanket of dark sky. A ring circled the moon—a sure sign rain was coming.

An ironic smile touched Roxey's lips. Four months ago, she'd never heard of the *Farmer's Almanac*, but it had been quoted so many times during her stay with the Dandridges that now its truisms were even echoed in her thoughts.

Her gaze drifted to the magnolia tree in the yard below and the swing swaying gently in the wind beneath it. How she yearned again for the night Seth had swung her there. To feel him lifting her, then cradling her in his lap, his arms tightening around her waist. To feel the strength of his chest against her back as she leaned into him. She closed her eyes and felt the movement of the swing, Seth's hands on her waist and the wind riffling through her hair.

Her chin dipped to her chest, her forehead touching the cool glass of the window as a tear coursed slowly down her face. It was only a memory, a dream to cling to in a lonely hour.

Muffled movements from downstairs told her Seth had returned from the barn. It was time. She slipped on her robe and quietly stole from her room so as not to wake the children. When she reached the bottom of the stairs, she saw a light shining beneath the kitchen door. Garnering her courage, she pushed open the swinging door and stepped into the room.

Seth stood at the sink, his shirt off and his jeans riding low on his waist. He touched his fingers to the water running at the faucet, then cupped his hands beneath it and bent forward, splashing the water over his face. With his eyes squeezed shut, he patted the counter top with his right hand, feeling around for the towel that lay just out of reach. Silently, Roxey tiptoed forward and placed the towel in his hand.

Seth cocked his head in her direction and squinted one eye at her. His mumbled "thanks" was barely audible through the towel as he briskly rubbed it across his face.

The afternoon's disastrous confrontation with Lorissa had left everyone in a quiet and pensive mood. Cissy had barely touched her dinner and had gone to bed early without a fuss. Brandon had eaten and slipped off to his room without so much as a good-night. Seth hadn't even appeared for dinner. He'd worked out in the barn, and when Roxey sent Brandon after him to tell him dinner was ready, Seth had sent back the message he wasn't hungry.

He was avoiding her. Roxey sensed it. Why did they insist upon punishing her for Lorissa's mistakes? First Brandon, and now Seth. It wasn't Roxey's fault Lorissa had left Seth and the children and moved back to the city. And it wasn't Roxey's fault Lorissa acted like some kind of china doll who wanted to be admired, but never touched.

Seth tossed down the towel and reached into the cupboard for a glass. "Figured you'd be in bed by now."

"I was just going." Roxey walked around the table to one of the ladder-back chairs pushed up to it and gripped its top rung in her hands.

"I wanted to let you know I'll be leaving tomorrow."

Seth's hand froze on the faucet handle, then relaxed as he twisted it and filled his glass with water. With his back still to her and his gaze centered on the dark kitchen window, he asked, "Why?"

"I can't do this anymore." She felt her lip begin to quiver and bit down on it. She couldn't allow herself to cry. "I've done everything I know to show you how much I love you, and I've tried my darnedest to overcome the obstacles between us. From the first, I've known that Brandon resented my presence here, but today I felt as if he and I had at last come to an understanding.

"You've said you're too old for me, but our age difference has never bothered me. And besides, there's nothing I can do to add years to my age, or take away any of yours."

She paused as she drew in a deep breath, willing herself to continue, to broach the one subject they'd never discussed. "And then there's Lorissa."

She watched the muscles on his back tense. At last, she'd reached a sore spot. "I'm not Lorissa, Seth. I don't know why you insist on judging me for her mistakes."

She waited for a moment for him to respond. To say something...anything! "Seth, please."

He set the glass down on the counter without ever having tasted the water and rested his palms against the counter top, continuing to stare out the kitchen window, his face taut and unyielding. "If you would, leave before the children wake up. It'll be easier that way."

Roxey staggered back as if he'd hit her. "Leave without saying goodbye to the children? Is that all you have to say? Why can't you let go of that damn stubborn streak and at least look at me?"

Seconds ticked by without Seth's moving so much as a muscle. Roxey wanted desperately to go to him and tear down that stubborn wall of indifference. If he would look at her, talk to her, she knew she could make him understand.

She stretched out a hand to him. "Seth, please..." But he remained at the sink, his back turned to her.

He loved her, Roxey knew he did. And she loved him. Oh, God, how she loved him. She'd risked everything in forcing this confrontation...and had lost it all. His presence in her life, his friendship...his love.

Grasping at what pride remained, Roxey drew her hand back to clutch tightly at the ladder-back chair. Her chin lifted unnaturally high, she whispered in a husky voice. "No, Seth. *I'm* no coward. I'll say goodbye to the children before I leave."

Thirteen

The first snow fell the second week of December, quickly covering the ground in a thick blanket of white. Knowing there was a good chance they could be snowbound and unable to get into town for a while, Seth loaded up the kids and headed for Miss Bertha's.

She met them at the back door, shooing the children in to sit by the fireplace while she made them some hot cocoa. Seth pulled up a chair at the kitchen table and drew a paper and pen from his coat pocket.

"I'm going into town. Is there anything you need?"

"Yes, as a matter of fact there is." Miss Bertha put the saucepan on the stove and adjusted the gas burner beneath it before joining Seth at the table. "Would you mind going by the fabric shop and picking me up more yarn?" She leaned over and dug around in the sewing basket beside her chair. When she straightened she held in her hands a sweater minus one sleeve. It was blue. The same blue as Roxey's eyes.

"I'm making this for Roxey for Christmas, and I ran out of yarn last night." She laid the wrapper from her last skein on the table. "The lot number is on here. Two more skeins ought to do me."

Reluctantly, Seth picked up the wrapper and quickly stuffed it in his pocket. "Anything else?"

Miss Bertha sat back against her chair, and folded her arms across her ample bosom. "Yes, you could call Roxey while you're in town."

Seth set his jaw and glared at Miss Bertha. "I've no need to talk to her."

"Humph. That's what you think. Ever since she left, you've been stomping around this farm like an old grizzly with a bee caught in his craw. Why don't you admit it, Seth? You love her and miss her as much as the rest of us."

Seth stood, his chair scraping against the floor in his haste to rise. "Leave it be, Miss Bertha."

"No, I *won't* leave it be. I've been quiet long enough. You're going to hear me out. I watched you shut yourself away on this farm when Lorissa left, and I never said a word. Figured you needed time to get over the hurt of her walking off. But by durn, this time you're the one doing the hurting. Roxey never did anything but open up her heart and love you and the kids. And what did you give her in return? Huh? Nothing! That's what. Nothing but grief.

"Just look at you. You haven't had a haircut in months. You don't even try to take care of yourself. What are you trying to prove? That you're not good enough for her? Well, maybe you *aren't* good enough for our Roxey. But don't kid yourself. It doesn't have anything to do with money or class."

Frustrated by his stony silence, she pushed up from the table and went to the stove to stir the cocoa. "I don't know why I'm wasting my breath on a stubborn old mule like you."

Miss Bertha's words continued to sting Seth as he sat in his truck in front of the fabric store. He pulled the piece of paper from his pocket and glanced at his scrawled list. After he drew a line through range pellets, only one item remained: the two skeins of yarn for Miss Bertha. A muscle ticked in his jaw as he remembered the tongue-lashing she'd given him. What did Miss Bertha know about anything anyway? Roxey was better off without him. He'd been right to let her go.

He dug his hand back into his pocket and pulled out the wrapper with the lot number for the yarn. A piece of blue fuzz was caught on the gummy label, and Seth picked if off and rolled it into a ball between his thumb and index finger. The scrap of yarn reminded him again of Roxey's eyes. He closed his fingers around the soft fuzz. God, he missed her. He hadn't allowed himself to admit that until now, but it was true. Without her, life on the farm had become drudgery, hardly worth the effort.

When he stepped from the truck, a sharp wind cut through him, pelting him with icy flakes of snow. He pulled up his collar against the wind and hurried to the sidewalk fronting the fabric store. In the wide storefront window, he caught a glimpse of himself and what he saw stopped him dead in his tracks. He looked like hell! The down coat he wore was stained with grease and ripped under one arm. The undershirt showing beneath his red flannel shirt was frayed and dingy.

He raked a hand through his hair in an attempt to shake the snow from it and tried to remember the last time he'd had a haircut. Not since he was in Louisville at Roxey's house when she'd sat on his lap while she trimmed it.

He dropped his hand to his beard and smoothed a hand over it, feeling its coarse unruliness. Miss Bertha had called him a stubborn mule. A rueful smile tugged at his mouth as he remembered the times Roxey had called him that same thing. The smile slowly faded. Even smiling wasn't worth the effort. Everything had lost its appeal without Roxey to share it with. And there wasn't a damn thing he could do about it.

He stared, frowning at his reflection a few moments before the muscles in his face began to tighten and his eyes to narrow. He raised his hands to his hips and glared back at his reflection in the window, his eyes sparking with new-found determination. He spun on his heel and headed down the sidewalk toward the red-and-white striped barber pole.

And only hoped he wasn't too late.

Five o'clock. Roxey refolded the computer sheets she'd been studying and slipped the financial report back into its file. Friday afternoon and another empty weekend stretched uninvitingly before her. Heaving a weary sigh, she locked her desk and switched off her office light.

Joanne, her secretary, was pulling the cover over her typewriter as Roxey passed by. "Are you calling it a day?" Joanne asked.

"Yes. Unless you need something."

"No. But your father stopped by a minute ago. He wanted to see you, but he was called back to his office to take a phone call before I had a chance to buzz you."

"I'll stop by his office on my way out. Have a good weekend, Joanne."

"You, too, Roxey."

Roxey walked down the hall to her father's spacious office and peeked around his door. He sat at his desk with the phone receiver pressed to his ear. By the frown he wore, Roxey suspected he wasn't very pleased with the person he was talking to.

She tapped lightly on the door and her father glanced up, then motioned for her to come in.

"What's wrong with the ski clothes you bought last year?" J.P. Classen pulled off his glasses and rubbed wearily at his eyes.

One side of the conversation was all Roxey needed to hear to know that her father was talking to Monica. She'd received a phone call from her sister earlier that day and had already heard about the *fabulously* rich man who had invited Monica to go skiing with him in Vale.

There was always a man in Monica's life. She went through them faster than Roxey did a box of tissues. Each one a little more handsome, a little richer than the one before. There were times when Roxey wished she were more like her older sister. Not that she required wealth or looks in a man, but she envied her sister her ability to forget. To move on when a relationship was at an end.

"All right, Monica. I'll put a couple of thousand in your account, but that's it until the first of the month."

J.P. Classen replaced the receiver and turned to Roxey. He forced a smile. "Glad you stopped by. I wanted to tell you how proud I am of the way you handled yourself at the loan meeting today."

Roxey lifted her shoulder in a shrug. "Just doing my job."

"All the same, you're to be commended. It was a questionable loan package, but you managed to win the approval of the board. Why don't we celebrate? Join your mother and I for dinner at the club."

Roxey shook her head. "Thanks, Dad, but I don't think so. I thought I'd pick up some Chinese food on my way home." She stood. "If that's all you needed—"

"No, as a matter of fact it isn't." J.P. stood and tossed his glasses onto his desk. "Your mother and I are worried about you, Roxey. You're unhappy and we feel somewhat responsible." Obviously ill at ease with the conversation, he scooped up some papers from his desk top and pushed them into a neat pile, avoiding Roxey's gaze. He cleared his throat. "We've always wanted what is best for you and Monica and sometimes in trying to achieve that goal we've made mistakes. Without meaning to, it seems we've burdened you with our expectations for your happiness.

"Your feelings for this Dandridge man took us by surprise. We had always assumed you'd choose someone within your own . . . well, to be blunt, your own social class. I had hoped by offering you the job in the bank, you would forget him. But it seems you haven't. If anything, you're more miserable than before."

Tears welled in Roxey's eyes. Miserable wasn't a strong enough word to express the emptiness she felt. But it wasn't her father's fault. He hadn't done anything to sever her relationship with Seth.

Catching her father's hand in hers, she offered him a tentative smile. "Don't blame yourself, Dad. It just wasn't meant to be."

He squeezed her hand between his. "I just want you to be happy, Roxey. That's all a father can ask."

The room was draped in shadows, the only illumination coming from the red glow on the stereo's control panel. Soft piano music flowed around the room from discreetly concealed speakers. Roxey lay on the sofa with one hand tucked beneath her cheek. She was in that drugged state—not quite asleep, yet not awake, either. In front of her on the coffee table sat small white boxes of Chinese carryout with the lids gaping open. A plastic fork stuck out of one, chopsticks from another.

Subconsciously, Roxey was aware of condensation pooling around a beer bottle. She knew it would leave a watermark on the dark wood of her coffee table, but she didn't have the energy to move it. She was tired. *So* tired.

She snuggled deeper into the cushions and allowed her mind to roam free, to carry her where it would. Today had been a good day. The first *really* good day in a long time. The approval of Russell Jackson's loan had lifted her spirits—if only for a moment. She felt a warm, satisfied glow spread through her as she remembered the look on Russell's face when she told him the news. Such a nice guy. He deserved the chance to prove himself.

The Chinese take-out had been her idea of a private, solitary celebration, but then Russell had unexpectedly appeared at her door with a six-pack of beer. She'd invited him to share her dinner, and in turn he'd shared his beer with her. They drank toasts to the success of the Rocking J Farm from long-neck beer bottles. Champagne would have been more to Roxey's taste, but, after all, it was Russell's celebration.

A bell sounded, and in her sleepy stupor, Roxey strained to place the sound, but soon gave up. It was too hard to think. She was exhausted. It was weeks since she'd slept well, and tonight her body demanded rest.

The bell sounded again, followed quickly by a pounding sound. Could someone be stuck on the office elevator? She tried to force her mind to focus. No, she wasn't at the office, so it couldn't be the elevator. Remembering she was home and lying on her sofa, she raised a heavy arm and batted futilely above her head for the phone she'd placed on the beveled glass sofa table. When her fingers at last rested on it, she pulled the receiver from its cradle and dragged the phone to her ear.

"Hello." While the dial tone hummed in her ear, the bell sounded again. Roxey forced herself upright, realizing the sound was the doorbell.

She staggered to the front door and closed her eyes as she leaned her cheek against the paneled wood. "Who is it?"

"Seth."

Her eyes flew open. Seth? Wide-awake, she stood on tiptoe and peered through the peephole. There was indeed a man on her stoop. His shoulders were hunched up against the cold, and his hands were stuffed deep into the side pockets of his jacket. He'd said he was Seth, but he certainly didn't look like him. She reached over and flipped on the porch light, not once moving her eye from the peephole.

Immediately, the man raised his hand to shade his eyes from the sudden bright light. His height was about right and he *did* sort of look like Seth.

She pulled the door open a crack. "Seth?"

"Hi." He smiled sheepishly as he drew his hand back from his eyes. "Hope I'm not disturbing you."

"No, no." She combed her fingers through her wild hair as she stepped back. "Please, come in." Steeling herself against the excitement his mere presence brought, she led the way into the living room, pausing to turn on a lamp before sinking onto the sofa. Seth glanced at the boxes of food and the empty beer bottles littering the coffee table and felt the first quiver of uncertainty.

He gestured to the mess. "A party?"

Roxey stood and slowly started gathering up the beer bottles. "No, just a little celebration. The board approved

Russell Jackson's loan today. You know. The one I told you about?''

"Oh, yeah." He felt a heaviness settle within his chest. Maybe he was too late after all. "Well, congratulations. I know how much getting that loan approved meant to you."

"Thanks." Roxey disposed of the bottles in the wastebasket behind the wet bar, then wiped the circles of water from the tabletop with a dry cloth. "Can I get you something to drink?"

"Bourbon'll be fine." He breathed out a nervous breath as he realized he needed something to fortify him.

Before handing him his glass, Roxey paused for a moment and frowned up at him. "What happened to your beard?"

Self-consciously, he rubbed his palm across his smooth jaw. "I shaved it off."

A glimmer of what he thought looked like regret sparked her eyes before she wrinkled her nose at him.

"For heaven's sake, why?"

This wasn't going at all as he'd planned. First of all he'd thought—or at least hoped—she would be thrilled to see him. He'd also thought the fact that he'd shaved would please her. But the only emotion she'd revealed upon his arrival was one of surprise, and the fact that he'd shaved, if anything, seemed to irritate her.

He took a sip of the smooth Kentucky bourbon, welcoming the burning sensation as it slid down his throat. With a forced casualness, he replied, "Oh, I don't know. Guess I just needed a change."

He sat down on the opposite end of the sofa from her.

"How are Cissy and Brandon?"

"Fine. Just fine."

"Where are they?"

"Well . . ." Seth cleared his throat and shifted nervously on the sofa. "They're at your parents'."

Roxey's eyes widened, and her mouth dropped open. "At my parents'! Why?"

"I went over there earlier tonight to talk to them, and they insisted I leave Cissy and Brandon there."

"Insisted? Mother? Come on, Seth. Is this some kind of joke?"

"No. It's no joke. But to be honest, I was a little surprised, too. When I left, your mother was having a tea party with Cissy, using real china cups, and your dad was challenging Brandon to a game of chess."

"Brandon doesn't stand a chance. Dad's a whiz at chess."

Seth laughed. "Don't count on it. Brandon's been beating me at chess since he was eight years old."

Realizing she'd allowed Seth to divert her attention from the subject at hand, Roxey asked, "Why did you take them over there?"

Seth leaned forward, cupping his glass between his hands as he swirled the amber liquid around the crystal tumbler. "I've been doing a lot of thinking, and I wanted to discuss a few things with your father before I talked to you."

Pushing his wrists against his thighs, he stood and strode to the bar and splashed another two fingers of bourbon into his glass. The glass shook slightly as he raised it to his lips. He quickly drained it. With his back to Roxey, he stared at the empty glass, unable to meet her gaze. He had a lot of explaining to do but was hard-pressed where to begin.

"Sometimes people do hurtful things to those they care the most for, thinking what they're doing is for the best. When you left the farm, I didn't try to stop you because I thought your leaving was for the best. The country life just didn't seem to be the life for you."

Every muscle in Roxey's body tensed as anger burned through her. For weeks she'd tried to prove to him she loved life in the country, as well as life with him. And for him to act on an assumption without even once considering what *she* wanted was just too much.

Seth set his glass on the bar and turned slowly to face her, stuffing his hands deep into the pockets of his slacks. "I knew when you left you were hurting, but I figured in time you'd see your leaving was the right decision."

He lowered his gaze to the Persian rug at his feet, then slowly lifted his eyes back to hers. The protective wall Roxey had built around herself was so thick it was almost visible.

If he tried to touch her, he knew he would never be able to penetrate it.

"I was a fool, Roxey. I see that now. I should've never let you go." His eyes burned with tightly held emotion. "But I did it because I loved you. You've got to believe that."

With her chin held high, she calmly replied. "No. You're wrong, Seth. You let me go because you were scared. Scared I would do to you what Lorissa did. Scared you might get hurt again. No, you never allowed yourself to love me, Seth. You were much too careful for that."

He absorbed her words, weighing each carefully. What she said was partly true. He'd loved her, he just hadn't allowed his love to show. He'd kept it all bundled up inside him. And now that he wanted to show her how much he cared, it looked as if he was too late. Her face remained taut and unforgiving.

Slowly he crossed the room, determined to close the distance between them, if only physically. Deep creases furrowed the narrow space between his brows as he sat down beside her and draped one arm on the sofa behind her.

"Part of what you say is true. I *was* scared. More scared than you'll ever know. But you're wrong if you think I don't love you. I do. It's just there was so much stacked against the chance of our ever being happy."

Roxey remained rigid beside him, refusing to look at him and unwilling to accept this unexpected change of heart. She had been vividly aware of every barrier stacked in their path, but she had loved him enough to chip away at those obstacles. Unfortunately, she'd found she could remove only those bricks on her side of the wall. Seth had erected his own defensive wall that she hadn't been able to breach. "So what's changed, Seth? You're still twelve years older than me. You still have two children, one of whom has a hard time accepting me. And my family is still filthy rich, something you can't quite forgive them." She turned to look at him, her face devoid of any emotion. "Their blue blood runs through my veins, too. So tell me, Seth. What's different?"

"Me." He said the word softly, simply, yet volumes of emotion were piled up under it. "*I've* changed." He clasped her hand in his, pulling it to his thigh and gripping it tightly. "Before you waltzed into our lives, I was perfectly content on the farm. I gave it my all, and in return, it gave me back my self-respect—something I'd lost when I lived in the city. It also provided a peaceful environment for me to raise my kids in. Then you came along, loving us and throwing sunshine on all our lives." He swallowed hard, his eyes burning bright as they looked deeply into hers. "Since you left, nothing's the same anymore. My life's empty without you, Roxey."

He squeezed her hand tightly in his. "I've decided to sell the farm and—"

"You can't—"

"I am. And I'm moving back to the city. I'll find a job here, something I can do without sacrificing my integrity. Cissy can go to the Dyslexic School and Brandon can go to a private school. And I want you to be a part of our lives again. I know I can't give you everything you're accustomed to, Roxey, but I'll give you the best I can provide."

With each revelation of his plans, anger built inside Roxey, growing until she thought she would burst. Finally, livid with suppressed fury, she jumped up, jerking her hand from his. She strode to the bar and flattened her palms against the cool counter top. With her elbows locked, she leaned her weight against the bar and waited a good thirty seconds before she wheeled to face him. "You have a lot of gall, you know that? Showing up on my doorstep without any warning after what you did to me. And how dare you presume what is best for me? How could you possibly know what is best or even what I want? You've never even bothered to ask."

She sucked in a deep breath and folded her arms tightly at her waist. "And what do my parents have to do with all this?"

Surprised by her anger, Seth at first just stared at her as she raved at him, then he leaned back against the sofa's cushioned back, his dimples deepening as he watched and listened. She had every right to be angry with him, and if it was just anger she was feeling, he knew there was still hope.

"In my generation, it's customary for a man to receive permission from a woman's family before he asks her to marry him."

"Oh, drop it, would you? I'm sick of hearing about the difference in our ages. And I don't need my parents' permission to marry. I'll marry who I want, when I want."

"Will you marry me?"

"No, I won't marry you, you stubborn mule!"

Seth laughed. Being called a mule didn't faze him. In fact, he kind of liked hearing her say it. It reminded him of other times when she'd call him that.

Her refusal of marriage didn't faze him, either. She loved him. Her anger proved him that, and he knew how to handle her anger. "What's wrong, Rox? You scared?"

"Scared? Of what?"

"Of me."

Indignant, Roxey dropped her arms to her sides, her hands pushed down in tight fists. "I'm not scared of you!"

"Then why don't you come and sit down beside me?"

"Because . . . because I'm mad at you."

He patted the sofa beside him. "If you're not scared, then you can be mad at me over here."

Roxey glared at him through narrowed eyes. He had her, and they both knew it. If she remained away, she was admitting she was scared. If she went to him, his touch would melt her anger. Well, two can play this game, she thought. She flounced over and flopped down beside him, sitting with her back ramrod straight and her palms pressed together on her lap, careful not to allow even so much as a thread on the fabric of her dress to brush against him.

He slipped his hand beneath the weight of her hair and gently squeezed the nape of her neck. His touch sent tingles shooting down her spine. Her eyes drifted closed as her shoulders started to sag, but she caught herself, forcing her eyes open and her back straight.

He chuckled softly. "I'm sorry you're mad, but you can get glad as fast as you got mad."

It was a phrase she'd heard him use with Cissy. It never failed to bring a smile to Cissy's face. Damn him! He just wasn't playing fair. Roxey propped her elbows on her knees and dropped her head, covering her face with her palms. Her anger was quickly dissipating, and she wasn't ready to let it go. Her voice was muffled by her fingertips. "I don't want to be glad. I'm not through being mad yet."

Seth chuckled and slipped his arm around her shoulders and pulled her back snug up against him. "Tell me what you want, Roxey. I promise I'll listen."

She took a deep shuddery breath, then released it, giving in to the comfort of his arms. A warmth quickly spilled into her heart, filling up the void she'd been living with since she left his farm weeks before.

Knowing that only with this man would she ever be complete, she tipped her head back to look at him. "I want you." She touched three fingertips to his smooth cheek. "But I don't want you to change for me. I want the Seth Dandridge I fell in love with."

He turned his lips into her palm, clasping her fingers in his.

Her eyes misted over. "Oh, Seth. Don't you see? I love *you*. Not for what you can be, but for what you are. Your farm, your children." She cupped his face in her hands as she smiled through her tears. "Even your beard. They're all a part of you, and I love them, too."

With her hands clasped in his, he turned, twisting Roxey around until they both sat sideways on the sofa, facing each other, their knees touching. "But what about your job? And the kids' schooling? You were right. I can't go on teaching them at home. There just isn't enough time in the day for all I have to do."

"Don't worry about my job. I can commute. And we can still enroll Cissy in the Dyslexic School and Brandon in a private school." She watched Seth's face cloud and knew immediately his thoughts. Quickly, she dispelled them.

"They wouldn't have to board there. They could ride into the city with me each day and home each—"

His lips silenced her as he grabbed her, pulling her into the fold of his arms. "Oh, Roxey. I love you."

"And I love you."

He brushed back her hair, framing her face with his hands while smoothing his thumbs along the hollow beneath her cheekbones. "Would you consider marrying this old mule-headed farmer?"

A smile slowly spread across Roxey's face. "Oh, yes."

He pulled her to him, wrapping his arms around her and hugging her tightly against his chest. Just as quickly he pushed away, gripping her shoulders with his hands, a broad smile splitting his face. "Let's go get the kids and tell them."

He started to stand, but she stopped him with a palm pressed against his chest. "There are a few conditions we need to discuss first."

"Conditions?" He frowned at her in confusion. "Like what?"

"First of all, Cissy and Brandon are *children* not kids."

Seth rolled his eyes heavenward and nodded his head, but before he could rise from the sofa, Roxey grabbed his arm. "Secondly, you have to install a phone in the house and in the barn." She smiled seductively before leaning against him and nuzzling his neck with her nose, sending pinpricks of desire prickling along his abdomen. "You never know when Cissy or Brandon or I might need to get in touch with you during the day."

"Agreed. Now let's go get—"

"Also—" she interrupted as she found his earlobe with her teeth and began to nibble "—you have to grow your beard back." She smoothed a hand across his cheek. "I like the feel of it rubbing against my skin when you kiss me."

Seth moaned when she nibbled at his earlobe then fought for sanity as she slipped her tongue into his ear, turning his stomach inside out. With his breathing growing more ragged by the second, Seth could only nod his agreement.

"And last but certainly not least—" Roxey eased her fingers between the buttons of his shirt and began to rake her fingernails across his chest "—we have to have the road to the house graded and rocked. I never want anything preventing me from getting home to you at night."

His husky "okay" was barely audible.

"Now—" she sat up, a pert smile on her lips "—let's go get the children."

With a mumbled oath that rumbled through his chest like a groan, Seth pushed Roxey down on the sofa, pinning her beneath him, capturing her lips in a wild assault of the senses. Like a thirsty man when at last given water, Seth drank deeply of Roxey's sweetness but found his thirst couldn't be satisfied with a simple kiss.

Feathering fevered kisses across her face, he breathed against her cheeks. "Do you think your parents would mind if the *children* stayed a little while longer?"

Roxey slipped her hands beneath his shirt and began to rub them seductively up and down his back. "They're going to be their grandparents, so they might as well get used to them."

His lips found hers again, slanting over hers, claiming her in a most satisfying, possessive way. Then suddenly they were gone. Roxey opened her eyes to find Seth had lifted himself above her. Worry lines wrinkled his forehead.

"What's wrong?"

"I just remembered the kids' last visit to your parents' home. God, what if they break something?"

"Don't worry," Roxey laughingly soothed as she pulled him back to her, locking her arms around Seth's neck. "Mom and Dad are insured."

* * * * *

 Silhouette Desire®

COMING
NEXT MONTH

#517 BEGINNER'S LUCK—Dixie Browning
Meet September's *Man of the Month*, Clement Barto. Mating habits:
unexplored. Women scared him speechless—literally. But with a little
beginner's luck, Clem was about to discover something called love....

#518 THE IDEAL MAN—Naomi Horton
Corporate headhunter Dani Ross had to find the right man for a client—
but the job title was "Husband." When she met rancher Jake Montana
she knew he was ideal—for her!

#519 ADAM'S WAY—Cathie Linz
Business efficiency expert Julia Trent insisted on a purely professional
relationship with problem-solver Adam MacKenzie. But he was
determined to make her see things Adam's way.

#520 ONCE IN LOVE WITH JESSIE—Sally Goldenbaum
Who says opposites don't attract? Confirmed bachelor Matt Ridgefield
had been content with his solitary life-style before carefree, spirited Jessie
Sager had come along. The professor had a lot to learn!

#521 ONE TOUCH OF MOONDUST—Sherryl Woods
Paul Reed was the most *romantic* man Gabrielle Clayton had ever met. He
was also her new roommate—and suddenly practical Gaby was dreaming
of moonlight and magic.

#522 A LIVING LEGEND—Nancy Martin
Hot on the trail of the scoop of the century, Catty Sinclair found only
gruff recluse Seth Bernstein. What *was* this gorgeous man doing in the
middle of nowhere...?

AVAILABLE NOW:

#511 MOUNTAIN MAN
Joyce Thies

#512 SQUEEZE PLAY
Anne Caviliere

#513 RACE THE WIND
Noreen Brownlie

#514 GALE FORCE
Jo Andrews

#515 A LITTLE BIT COUNTRY
Peggy Moreland

#516 JUST KATE
Linda Lael Miller